How Still My Love

a contemporary romance

How Still My Love

© 2017, 2014 by Diane Marina

This electronic original is published by Aspen Palms Press, New Market, Maryland, USA.

This is a work of fiction. Names, characters, places and incidents are the product of the author's imagination or are used fictitiously. Any resemblance to actual persons, living or dead, is completely coincidental.

This book, or parts thereof, may not be reproduced in any form without permission from the author.

CREDITS

Editing: Day Petersen

Acknowledgments

For my wife, Angela, who has traveled with me every step of the way to finish this book and to have it published the way it was meant to be. Thank you for your constant support, love and encouragement.

For all of those who read this for me and gave me valuable feedback to make it a better story – Suzie Carr, Joanna Jasmin Darrell, Joni Bayes, Melissa Campbell, Di Manning, and Kathy King – thank you so much.

Special thanks to Suzie Carr for your guidance along the way. You never hesitate to give input or share your knowledge, and I value your friendship. Saying "thank you" a million times could never be enough to voice my appreciation.

Thanks to Day Petersen for molding the story into its final form. Your input, as always was the frosting on the cake.

How Still My Love – a contemporary romance

Chapter One

    As I leaned forward in my office chair, the supple leather gave way with my movements. I tapped my pen on the desk and surveyed the financial statements from the last quarter. My design studio, still young enough to be struggling, had been profitable so far this year, a fact that brought a smile to my face. I was jotting myself a note to give the staff some sort of bonus in appreciation, when I heard murmurs outside my office in the main studio. Voices raised in greeting and laughter added to the usual background noise of phones ringing and printers printing. I heard the click clack of heels come toward my office, and I knew it could only be one person.

    Laurel charged through my office door and made a beeline for my desk. Her job as a high school art teacher gave her some flexibility to drop into my design studio when the mood struck her, as long as that mood struck on school holidays. In this instance, it was Spring Break.

    I wasn't alarmed by the raging-bull-on-speed routine, as it was her typical behavior when she had something to share. I heard her the second she entered my studio, and knew she would make a grand entrance into my office, whatever it turned out to be. I loved Laurel, but saying she was a drama queen was like saying Elvis was a singer.

Laurel moved from the door to my desk in three quick strides — her long legs capturing my attention, as usual — and grabbed the arms of my chair, rolling me away from my desk. The chair did a half-spin and slammed into the wall with me in it.

"Ow! Hey, what the hell are you doing?" I was a little miffed at the interruption as well as the physical means Laurel sometimes used to get my attention. I rubbed my elbow, which had grazed the wall. *Damn. That really did smart.* "You've finally gone insane, haven't you? I knew the day was coming."

"What have you got planned for Friday night?" Laurel's arms were folded across her chest, and her bright pink nails tapped on her biceps. With her eyes narrowed, I could barely see her bright green eyes as they studied me from beneath her lashes.

"Stop trying to read my mind. I hate when you do that." I rolled back to my desk and resumed scrolling through my email.

She quit staring at me and perched on the edge of my desk. From the corner of my eye, I could see that she was twirling her hair around her finger while she waited for my answer. I considered not responding, but I knew that would only prolong *my* agony.

"See? Absolutely nothing." When I didn't immediately refute her assertion, she assumed that it was correct, and she continued, ignoring the fact that I was ignoring her. "Just as I suspected. You have no excuse not to go."

Laurel is my oldest and closest friend, and sometimes my worst enemy. I hate when she puts herself in the "bossy big sister" role she plays so well. Despite knowing it was exactly what she wanted me to do, and in no mood to comply with her wishes, I glanced up.

"Go where, Laurel? You know, if you would conduct yourself like a normal person, things would be much easier on both of us." I minimized my email screen and leaned back in my chair. "Most people, myself included, would have come in, said 'hi, how have you been? I have a great idea. What are your plans for the weekend?' But no, you have to come barreling in here and slam me against a wall. What kind of friend does *that*? Will should have you committed."

She wore a smug grin, and damn, she looked sexy.

When I looked at Laurel, I couldn't help noticing anew how attractive she was, even prettier than when we had been in art school together. I'd be the first to admit, but only to myself, that I had a long-standing crush on my best friend. If it wasn't for her pushy personality, I might even have fallen in love with her. Thank God for imperfections.

"Laurel, my bills aren't going to pay themselves," I said with a sigh. "My staff expects to be paid, and that won't happen if you don't let me get back to work."

She swung her leg and tapped her pointy-toed shoe against my calf. "I found a lesbian for you."

My mouth dropped open, and I blinked at her. "Oh. Okay, good, because I've been looking for one. You know how I love to accessorize." I tried not to laugh. "They're so hard to find on E-Bay these days."

"Beth, come on. Time to drop the 'no dating' policy. It doesn't suit you. It's a friend from work. I've finally convinced her to go out with you." Laurel beamed at me, apparently proud of her perceived accomplishment.

I rested my elbow on the arm of my chair and settled my chin on my palm. "No. Not that you haven't made the offer *extremely* appealing, but no. You know my policy — business first, pleasure second. My business still needs my constant attention, and I'm not ready to go down the dating road just yet."

"You're not going to get any work done until I leave, and I'm not leaving until you say 'yes.'" She grinned triumphantly, and I felt annoyance brewing.

Laurel knew my history. She had lived through it with me. I'd been burned, and burned badly. It had been years since I had dated anyone, and it would be a lot longer before I would consider dating again. Having fun with a hot woman every once in a while was one thing, and I was certainly no stranger to that, but I was not in the market for a relationship. Now my only love was my company. I pressed my palms on my burning cheeks and tried to maintain my cool.

Sounds of movement in the main studio, just outside my office, told me that my lead designer had returned from his lunch break. Bryce wore noisier heels than any pair of high heels I'd ever come across.

Laurel heard too, and her head twitched in the general direction of the open studio. Her mouth opened slightly.

Propelled by the prospect of being outnumbered, I sprang from my chair and grasped her shoulders before she could call

Bryce's name, but she shrugged my hands aside and went to the doorway.

"No, no, no, no, no. Laurel, no. Do not involve—" Before I could finish, she was at the door, asking Bryce to join us.

His large, muscular figure filled my doorway, his mouth upturned in a wide smile from the recesses of his graying goatee. He was as pretty as a man could be, and he flaunted it. The pinstriped vest over a meticulously pressed, button-down shirt made him look almost regal. He greeted Laurel with a warm hug.

"Whatever you are trying to convince the boss to do, I'll help," he offered devilishly.

I flopped into my chair. Bryce and Laurel got on well together, and this was a game they enjoyed playing. Whenever Laurel wanted me to do something, Bryce was usually in her court. The fight was now two against one, and I was undoubtedly on the losing side.

"I'm trying to set up two beautiful, intelligent, kind women on a date, but one of them is being stubborn about not letting me do it."

Bryce tsked and tapped his chin while he looked at me with blatant disapproval.

"Oh no." I rolled my eyes, rested my face in my hands, and groaned. My annoyance was morphing into resignation. I knew they thought they were ganging up on me for a good reason.

"What's wrong with you?" Bryce admonished, his crystal blue eyes dancing, despite his tone. "I'd be honored if Laurel would find a handsome young gentleman for me to date. Hint,

hint." He winked in Laurel's direction. "It's not like she's selling you into an arranged marriage or some such nonsense!"

Oh God, did he just say that out loud? Stop giving Laurel ideas!

Bryce had made his point. It was my turn to glare.

Lord help me. "Name one couple that is together today as the result of a blind date," I challenged.

"Will and me," Laurel replied without missing a beat.

"You liar! I happen to know you stalked that poor guy until he finally asked you out. There are days he's still sorry he gave in. The only reason he married you is because you hounded him so relentlessly, it was the only way he could get any peace and quiet. Little did he know *that* would never come."

Ignoring my jibe, Laurel switched tactics. "Look, you won't be alone. Will and I have a babysitter lined up, and we'll be with you. Come on. You know we never get out any more. I need this double date more than you do. Do it for me," she pleaded.

She smiled her perfect smile filled with perfect white teeth, and I had a fleeting vision of darkening some of them in with a Sharpie. I went so far as to glance around my desk, but all I found was a highlighter. *Hmmm.*

"Beth," she whined.

No, no, no. This was not something I wanted to deal with. It had taken years for the wounds from my last relationship to heal; my heart was still scarred. I was happy with the status quo.

"Fine. I'll be your babysitter, and then you and Will can have an evening out alone. Or if you really feel the need to provide an evening out for this work friend of yours, have her babysit for you. Then you and I will *both* be happy," I suggested, anger beginning to bubble in my chest. "You know how I feel about this, Laurel. Don't push me."

"I know Toni well. She's a good friend of mine."

"Since when? You don't have any good friends that I don't know. Funny how I'm just now hearing about this *good* friend."

"The two of you will get along, I know you will." She was pleading now. "She's your type, trust me."

"What is that supposed to mean?" I didn't even have a type, or at least I wasn't aware of what my type was besides female. "Oh, wait. You've found 'a lesbian' for me. I guess, to you, that's my type."

At that point, my assistant, phone answerer, and all-around crisis-solver walked into my office. Kristy took in the look on my face and turned to Bryce. "What am I missing?"

Bryce nodded at me. "She's refusing to go on a date with the woman of her dreams."

Oh geez. I shot him a pointed look. "Want to keep your job?"

"Ooooh, details. I want details! Why are you refusing? What's the big deal, Beth?" Kristy asked. "Dates don't last forever. If it doesn't go well, you can call it an early night. Or have Laurel call you mid-date with an unexpected emergency, in case you need an excuse to cut out."

"Kristy, you missed the best part of the deal," I said. "I get to spend the evening with Laurel, too. Apparently double dates are all the rage with the thirty-something crowd."

Kristy guffawed. She was the only one in the office who truly appreciated my sarcastic bent and showed it with her bellowing laughter. How such a tiny girl could emit such a booming laugh, I'd never know.

"Well, to be fair to Laurel, you have to admit that you haven't gone out with anyone in the entire time I've known you. It's time." Kristy nodded. Her agreeing with Laurel only rubbed salt in the wound.

My cheeks burned as I thought about some of my one-night stands. *If she only knew.* It was easy for her to dole out dating advice, considering she'd been living in bliss with the same man for the last four years.

"That's right," Laurel agreed, taking her turn at wearing me down. "As a matter of fact, there hasn't been anyone serious since Julie. And that was how many years ago?"

My anger at Laurel ramped up a notch, and I bit my lip to hold in an angry response. She knew what Julie had done to me, physically and emotionally. I folded my arms across my chest and tried to banish the thought of Julie from my mind. When I felt more in control, I said, "I haven't thought about her in a while, which explains why I've been sleeping so soundly. Why on earth did you bring her up?"

"My point is that you found Julie yourself. Please give me a chance to find someone who's right for you." Laurel moved closer to me and placed her hand on my arm. "Beth, it's time, sweetie. Don't let that…that troll keep you from finding someone wonderful. I have never tried to set you up before, but believe me, Toni's smart, beautiful, funny, and truly a good person. I wouldn't let just anyone go out with my best friend."

And there stood the reason Laurel was my best friend. She could push me to the brink of madness, but her genuine concern for me and her big heart always won out. She loved me like no other. I knew that I would have to give in to her wishes.

I leaned back in my seat and ran my hands through my hair. Everyone was watching me, waiting for a response. Laurel moved closer, eyes pleading.

I surrendered. "Ohhh…okay."

Applause and cheers erupted around me as I got up to usher everyone from my office. The smile on Laurel's face was brilliant, and my stomach took a pleasant roll.

"All right, you've gotten your way, now leave." My stomach rumbled, and I looked at my watch and scowled. "I have a meeting with a client in fifteen minutes, so please, get out of here so I can get something to eat before then."

Bryce and Kristy wisely returned to their desks. I walked Laurel out through the open area where the staff worked, to the large, industrial door that was the entrance to the studio.

"I told Will I'd be home by two, but I can set the whole thing up tonight if you're sure you mean it," Laurel said excitedly. "You're not going to rethink this and then back out, are you?" Her left eye twitched.

I thought I detected a trace of nervousness on her face, and realized that I enjoyed the possibility after the agony she had put me through. I came close to telling her that I was already having second thoughts, just to worry her, but before I could reply, Bryce called out, "Don't worry, sweetie, I won't let her change her mind."

I tossed him a glare that was a clear warning for him to get back to work. I opened the door and pointed, then waited for Laurel to exit.

She kissed my cheek. "I'll call you tonight, Beth."

After a final wave, she disappeared around the corner of the hallway. I took great pleasure in closing the heavy door behind her. When I spun around to go back to my office, I found Bryce and Kristy watching me intently.

"What are you going to wear?" Kristy asked.

"I don't have any idea, and I'm certainly not going to worry about it, since this is only Monday." I stalked into my office and slammed the door.

I pulled my desk drawer open and rummaged through it until I found a package of crackers. I ripped open the cellophane and leaned back in my chair, eating each one carefully so as to minimize crumbs. I willed myself to relax before my client arrived.

For two years, I had been throwing all of my energy into getting my design studio off the ground. I'd put so much into the business that I hadn't taken any time for myself, and I was lonely. I knew that I would eventually have to open myself up to a new relationship, but the hazards terrified me.

Julie had been abusive. Our last night together ended with a call to the police and me moving my belongings into a friend's apartment. The only good memory I had of the entire rotten situation was of Laurel holding me and stroking my hair in an attempt to comfort me, which was the beginning of my crush on my best friend.

On top of the stress and heartache with Julie, I hated the job I had then. I was putting in long hours at an agency that I knew would not reward me for my efforts, and I was utterly drained. When I decided I'd had enough of my life in Philadelphia and needed a clean start, Laurel convinced me to move to the busy and surprisingly fun town of Frederick, Maryland, where she and Will had settled post-grad school. I left Pennsylvania behind and never looked back.

I shook myself out of the past, stretched, and went to my office window. The return of spring was present in the trees outside. I could see little pops of green, and some yellow here and there as the forsythia raced to beat all the other shrubs into bloom. I thought about Friday. Despite a budding anticipation as to what the evening might bring, I suppressed any hope that this friend of Laurel's could turn into the real thing for me. Besides, living with a secret crush on a straight woman was so much easier than dealing with life's realities. I told myself that if nothing did come of the date, I'd be perfectly happy with the status quo.

Laurel hadn't told me a thing about this woman, apart from her name and why she thought we'd be a perfect match. I just hoped for the best, which would be a pleasant evening out with old friends and possibly a new one. At least Laurel and Will would be there to fill any lulls in the conversation if the evening was a disaster.

I heard a soft knock, but before I could respond, Kristy flung the door open.

"Beth, this is Kara Winters. Ms. Winters, I'll be right in with your coffee."

As I stood and greeted the new client, I consciously swept away the images conjured up during the previous hour and focused on work.

Chapter Two

I paced my living room with my phone pressed against my ear, grilling Laurel about the impending date. "All right, what's wrong with this woman? Has she just been released from a mental institution? That must be it! My luck always runs in the direction of psychiatric illness. In fact, it's not even a coincidence anymore, but a given." I stopped and studied my nails while I waited for her response. I noted that I desperately needed a manicure.

"Give me a break!" Laurel groaned. "Do you honestly think I'd set you up with someone like that?"

I envisioned my friend on the other end of the line. I was sure she had just stomped her foot. The thought made me smile. We could both be so juvenile.

"You might not do it intentionally," I allowed. I was still suspicious as to why I hadn't heard about this friend sooner.

"Well then, why don't you come over for dinner tonight," she offered, "and I'll convince you that you've made the right decision."

I stopped pacing and rubbed my tired eyes while I considered her offer. I've always told Laurel that she was in the wrong profession. She would have made a wonderful salesperson. If she'd gone into auto sales, I'd have more cars than Jay Leno. My feet were aching, and I wanted nothing more than to jump into a hot bath and then slip into an old pair of jeans. Going out was not on my list of Top Ten Things To Do For The Evening, but I knew Laurel would be stubborn about it. Besides, I wanted to know more about this mystery woman, and going to Laurel and Will's also meant I didn't have to make dinner. The crackers I'd had that afternoon were the only thing I'd eaten since breakfast.

"Can I take a shower first?"

"God, please do!" She laughed at her own joke. "Will isn't home yet anyway. See you in about an hour and a half?"

After we hung up, I kicked my heels off and headed for the bathroom. With the water on full force and as hot as I could stand it, I stripped off my clothes and jumped into the shower. Under the stream blasting on the back of my neck, I felt the day's tension gradually seeping from my body.

I stepped from the shower and patted myself dry with a fluffy towel. Checking the time, I estimated that I had forty-five minutes to get to Laurel's. I towel-dried my hair and slipped on my favorite jeans and a soft, long-sleeved Henley.

I did a quick quality check in the mirror to make sure I could be seen in public without embarrassing myself. I noticed a smudge of makeup that hadn't come off in the shower. Nothing a little spit bath couldn't fix. I licked my forefinger and went to work on the smear. Next I checked my teeth to make sure there was no evidence of the crackers I'd had for lunch lodged in between them. Perfect and white, as always, and the one thing I could thank my parents for. I took a moment to study myself in the mirror. No wrinkles yet, except for a few laugh lines that were beginning to form around my eyes. I ran my fingers through my hair, twirling a few strands with my finger to bring out the natural wave. No gray hairs yet. My gray eyes were still my best feature. Although I'd always considered them oddly-tinted, Laurel called them my lady killers. My prominent cheekbones rarely needed any makeup. I tilted my head, trying to see myself for the first time as my date would in just a few days. I was satisfied that I was at least acceptable.

I ran down the loft stairs and grabbed my car keys from a table near the front door. I bopped out to the car, feeling better about myself and more energetic than I had in weeks. Maybe this unexpected matchmaking *was* what I needed.

I arrived at Laurel's house with ten minutes to spare. As I pulled into the driveway of their cozy suburban home, I spotted Becca, eight years old, and Kira, almost eleven, playing on the front lawn. They wore matching spring jackets. Laurel's husband Will was watching over them from the porch. He waved when he saw me, and laughed as the girls ran toward my parked car, squealing happily. I waved in his direction, thinking as I did every time I saw him that he reminded me of Keith Urban, without the shaggy hair. His face sported a small amount of scruff, and I wondered how Laurel could stand cuddling up to sandpaper.

"I brought something for dessert," I told the girls, holding up the brown paper bag with the ice cream I'd stopped to purchase on the way over. This sent them into fresh shrieks of excitement, which made me chuckle. The kids didn't even know what was in the bag, but that didn't matter.

"Hi, there." As I stepped onto the porch, Will kissed my cheek and his stubble brushed against it. "We haven't seen you in a while," he joked, having seen me just a few days before.

"If you saw me any more often, I'd be living here. You need a shave," I said.

He laughed and held the door for me to step into the house. He called to the girls and waited for them to barrel past him through the front door to the house before he followed us inside.

"You sound like Laurel. It's like I have two wives." He wiggled his eyebrows lasciviously.

"Well, you know, Laurel has trained me well." I said, rubbing my cheek. He really *did* need a shave. I moved into the living room and eyed my surroundings suspiciously. "There's no one besides your family here, is there?"

"Who else would be here?" Will asked.

"With your wife, one never knows."

As if on cue, Laurel walked into the living room, wiping her hands on a dishtowel. "What?" she asked, looking genuinely puzzled by the look I was giving her.

"I was just about to tell Will that as I walked into the house with my damp hair and torn jeans, I suddenly had a feeling that you might have invited a certain someone to join us in case I was to back out before Friday." My eyes darted around the room as I spoke, looking for a stranger to appear.

"I wouldn't do that. I know what you look like when you come over for dinner. I want you to make a good impression when you meet Toni, not scare her away." Laurel laughed as she tossed the towel in my direction.

I caught it before it could snap me in the head. My elbow still hurt from the thumping it had taken earlier, I wasn't about to let her injure me again.

"Thanks." I threw the towel back at her and headed for the kitchen to deposit the ice cream in the freezer. Laurel followed closely behind and eyed me steadily as she leaned against a counter.

"You're such a confidence booster," I said as I closed the freezer door and sat down at the table.

"Don't expect pity from me. I wish I looked as good as you do at your worst," Laurel said. "I'm glad you never competed with me for guys."

She was being kind, and she knew it. Although shorter in stature than me, she was just as thin. Her shorter hair was a bit darker than my golden blonde, but she was definitely as pretty as she claimed I was, if not more so.

Will came in and sat at the nearby island. "Well, if you two find each other so damned attractive, I say go for it."

Laurel and I both rolled our eyes. She moved behind Will and wrapped her arms around him.

"Stop it," I said to Will. "You," I nodded at Laurel, "tell me about her."

"Umm, who?" Laurel asked with feigned innocence.

"How quickly they forget. This person, this woman, this Toni you're forcing me to go out with on Friday."

"She's been trying to set you up with Toni all school year,"

Will supplied, rubbing a palm over his stubble.

It struck me then that the name sounded vaguely familiar. I thought that perhaps I did recall Laurel talking about her at some point, but her sexual orientation was never mentioned. That, I would have remembered. I hoped her lesbianism wasn't a recent self-discovery on Toni's part. That I could do without.

"She's very nice," Will offered as he joined us at the table. "I think you'll like her. Good thinking, Laurel. I wouldn't even have thought to set her up with Beth."

Laurel ran her hands over Will's shoulders. "That's because I'm a woman, and you're not. As a man, you might fantasize about the two of them together, but you wouldn't think to set them up first." She poked his back.

I made a face at the image her statement had conjured.

"She works with us at the school," Laurel said, as if that told me all I needed to know about the woman.

She went to the stove to check on whatever dish was filling the kitchen with a wonderful aroma. My stomach grumbled, distracting me from my intention of grilling her some more.

"We've become fairly good friends over the last few months, and she told me about her ex, who just happens to be a woman. Toni's very open about it at school," Laurel explained over the excited chatter of her children. "She's been over here for dinner a few times, and we've been to her place. I told her all about you. If it's any consolation, I had to twist her arm, too, until Will showed her photos of you."

"She saw photos of me? That doesn't really seem fair, does it?"

"She liked what she saw." Will grinned widely, showing way too many teeth.

"Show me a photo of her," I demanded.

"I don't think we have one." Laurel looked at her husband for verification. He dutifully nodded.

"What does she look like?" I prodded, looking in Will's direction. I felt petty for being so concerned about the woman's physical attributes, but what if she had a hideous laugh or voted Republican in the last election? I had to know more. I knew Will would give me a more honest description than his wife would.

"Ooooh, she's hot."

Laurel embellished a bit. "Trust me, Beth. She's beautiful, intelligent, funny. She loves the kids, she's a great cook — all the things you love. Stop doubting my judgment."

She looked at me in such a way that I knew the subject was closed. I could sit there and cajole her all night and she wouldn't tell me anything more, and I thought I knew why. Laurel wanted me to go into the evening without any preconceptions. She must have had a hard time getting her friend to agree to go out with me if she had to resort to showing her a photo, I thought with a hint of self-pity. So much for the empowering glance in the mirror earlier.

"I suppose I'll have to wait for Friday to find out anything else," I groused.

"I guess you will," Laurel answered, a smile of victory on her face.

Now I was not only curious, but actually looking forward to

this date. The way I saw it, Laurel was acting so secretive either because there was something terribly wrong with this woman and she'd taken pity on her, or she was the woman I'd been waiting for and Laurel knew it. Either way, it would make for an interesting evening.

What would Toni look like? Maybe she'd show up wearing an eye patch. *Too creepy.* Maybe she'd have tattoos and multiple piercings in her face. *Nah.*

A glass of sangria was placed before me, shaking me from my musings. Sangria could usually clear my head of many thoughts.

"Can you at least tell me where we're going, so I'll dress appropriately?

Will shrugged. He had no delusions of having any control of the situation.

"I thought we could go to dinner downtown. Maybe *Acacia*, because it's not too fancy, but not too casual, either. Your wardrobe consists of jeans, t-shirts, and business attire, nothing in between. None of those will do, I'm afraid. Tomorrow afternoon, we need to go shopping for something for you to wear."

Wow. My best friend had just morphed into my mother, but in a "good mom" sort of way. I sighed in resignation. It was clear who was in charge of Friday evening. I hoped it wouldn't be a waste of my time and money.

Chapter Three

Even in the dead of winter, Frederick is a beautiful city, but on this early spring afternoon, it was absolutely gorgeous, with a brilliant warm sun and just a hint of brisk chill in the air. At every turn, ornate church spires are visible, and the streets are framed with businesses and homes in a mish-mosh of architectural styles. The downtown shopping area is surrounded by historic buildings, some that survived the Civil War, and the city overflows with independently owned shops. After my arrival, I quickly assimilated and became a diehard local. Nothing could make me move from my chosen hometown.

People were out in droves enjoying the perfect weather, and I was in high spirits. Nothing could ruin my mood, not even dress shopping with Laurel. I tucked my hands into the pockets of my jacket and tilted my head up, letting the sun warm my face.

Stops in two shops had gotten us no closer to finding the dress Laurel had in mind for me. Laurel and I chatted as we strolled along, stopping to look in the windows of each store we passed, usually only long enough for Laurel to disapprove of what she saw. Mid-sentence, something in a window caught her eye, and she grabbed my wrist and tugged me across the busy street.

"Let's go into this one." Laurel pulled me into yet another women's boutique, with plans to vicariously spend my money.

"You know," I began as I followed her, "I resent you tossing around insults about my wardrobe last night. There's absolutely nothing wrong with what I wear."

"I know." She patted my arm. "I just want you to be a knockout." She slid her sunglasses up onto her head and then began sorting through the dress rack.

"I already am," I teased.

She stopped looking at clothes and studied me as if she had just noticed I was with her. "Are you nervous? You're being wittier than usual, and you usually do that to hide your nervousness."

"No, no, I'm fine. I've bought dresses before. Nothing to be nervous about." I smiled, but her perturbed expression warned me that I should answer her question seriously.

I sighed. "Yes, of course I'm nervous. I'm going out with someone I know nothing about, you're picking out my clothing as well as deciding where we're going, and I haven't been on a date in oh, I don't know, five years. I don't even know how to talk to a woman anymore, let alone date one. I will probably just be an observer the entire evening. I feel like I'm being forced into an arranged marriage or being sold as a prime cut of beef. Are we off to build my dowry next?"

Laurel laughed. "Wow, okay. Well, let it all out, I guess." She tucked her hair behind her ear and circled around to my side of the rack. "Come on, don't be that way," she said as she steered me toward other dress racks. "I know deep down you're excited, but you're just being stubborn because you won't admit I may be right about this." She smiled, and an irresistible single dimple appeared in her left cheek.

I smiled in spite of myself.

"Don't forget, you won't be alone. We'll all have a great time together, I swear to you. It'll just be a fun night out with friends." She watched as I distractedly removed a dress from a nearby rack. "No. No, definitely not. You're not going with black, nothing so morose. You should be wearing burgundies and midnight blues. You need to accentuate your eyes. Didn't you learn anything about color in art school? You were there with me, right? Was I the only one paying attention?"

She moved away from me as she spoke, and I followed, sighing, which she ignored. I heard her shriek as a dress caught her eye, and she pulled me off in another direction.

"This is perfect!" she announced, holding the deep plum colored dress like a trophy. The color was gorgeous. I eyed it closely, admiring her taste. The short linen dress had three quarter sleeves, and looked as if it would hug me in all the right spots.

"This dress could work for any occasion. You could even wear it for work."

"You're beginning to sound a little too much like Tim Gunn for my taste, Laurel. Maybe even borderline Martha Stewart." I took the dress from her and held it at arm's length, admiring it. I had to admit I loved the dress, which was basic enough for me to wear to the studio, but elegant enough to meet with Laurel's approval.

"This is the one we've been looking for, Beth. Try it on."

The one we've *been looking for?* Carrying the dress over my shoulder, I headed for the dressing rooms. Inside, I slipped into the garment. "Perfect fit," I called out to Laurel, turning to catch my reflection. The plum color contrasted nicely with the gray of my eyes. I smiled at myself in the mirror.

"Let me see," she called through the door.

I opened it and stepped out, then spun to give her the full effect.

"It's perfect! I love this dress," she concluded.

"So do I," I admitted with a smile.

I re-entered the dressing room and studied myself in the mirror. Laurel was right. The dress was perfect. Feeling butterflies for the first time since Laurel had initiated her plan, I was beginning to look forward to Friday night.

"Now get your clothes back on and let's go. You're treating me to lunch," Laurel said through the door.

Chapter Four

    I sat at my desk, doodling on my ever-present sketchpad. Most of our designs came from the computer, but I still liked to get back to basics and draw to keep the ideas flowing. I began to sketch out a layout for a photographer client's new website, but my mind wandered, and my sketch soon became one that I drew often. My pencil moved rapidly, and a pair of woman's eyes emerged from the paper. Bold and dramatic, they were mesmerizing and gazed right into me. They didn't belong to anyone in particular, but they did remind me of Laurel's, just in the curve of the lid. I stopped and dropped the pencil on the pad with a thwap. I did some neck rolls to relieve some of the tension there, balled up the paper and threw it at the recycle bin across the room. It missed, as always, and I had to get up to pick it up and throw it away. It was my conscious attempt to not sit at my desk all day. The knot in my neck told me I had been doing so for too long.

    I stood at my office window and watched people passing by on the sidewalk outside. I thought about my sketch. Mindless scribbling was something I did when loneliness settled in, which was far too often lately. As much as opening myself up to love and intimacy scared me, it was something I craved.

I had managed to keep my Friday date deep in the recesses of my mind for much of the week while I concentrated on what I considered the real world. I wasn't about to ignore my work because of a date, even if it was my first date in years. Staying focused had been my mantra for years, and I'd vowed to never let that change. But this woman, whom I'd never met, was distracting me.

Keeping busy was the only solution. I'd recently acquired three new accounts and was putting in some extra hours to make sure we did the best job possible for our new clients while keeping the current clients happy. It helped me keep my mind off of the nervousness I felt building in me.

Not surprisingly, everyone around me kept reminding me of my upcoming date, until I demanded that they get lives of their own to concentrate on. I came to the conclusion that Bryce and Kristy's own existences were so dull that they felt the need to turn my life into their own personal soap opera.

I turned away from the window and grabbed my sunglasses. I needed a quick walk to limber up my joints and clear my head.

~ ~ ~

Friday came a little too quickly for me. Always in the back of my mind was the knowledge that I had this date hanging over me. My brain knew that it was nothing to worry about, but my heart thudded an extra beat whenever I thought about how my toxic relationship with Julie had been. That had started out like any other relationship — fun, loving, and wonderful, and then it slowly turned into something that I had to escape from to stay physically and emotionally healthy. Part of me was worried that could happen again.

I kept to myself most of the day, even though the office seemed more chaotic than on a typical Friday. Laurel called during lunch time to make sure I didn't plan to back out at the last minute. I had to admit that the thought had crossed my mind several times, but I promised myself that I wouldn't give in to any sudden impulses, especially since I cherished Laurel's friendship, most of the time.

"Don't worry," I assured her. "I'll be there at eight."

Lauren sputtered and squeaked, "The reservation is for seven!"

I laughed, always eager to tease Laurel. "I know that. I was having some fun with you. You don't have to hold my hand all the way. I've made it this far without a babysitter," I said, visions of Bryce and Kristy as unofficial babysitters floating in my head.

As if still not completely convinced of my sincerity, Laurel threatened me in a deep growl, "I'll never forgive you if you don't show up."

Her gruff voice created a ripple of pleasure in my belly. "Wow, turning butch on me?"

But I knew she was dead serious. Her loyalty was to me, but she also had to consider her friendship with Toni, and I knew not to put that in jeopardy.

Her silence told me she was not amused.

"You think I don't already know that?" I laughed. It came out more like a gurgle. "See you tonight," I said, hanging up before she could add any more threats.

I sat back in my chair and chewed on a hangnail. For the first time since the date was arranged, I found it difficult to keep my mind on work. My tension was immediately apparent to Bryce when he appeared in my doorway toward quitting time. He didn't hesitate to tease me.

"What time would you like me to have the U-Haul at your place tomorrow?" he asked, leaning in my doorway. His expression was so serious that I didn't catch on to his little joke until I heard Kristy giggling at her desk out in the main area.

I should have been on high alert for such comments, since earlier he had called me over to his computer monitor to look at some wedding invitations he had designed for me on his lunch break. If I didn't feel as much affection as I did for him, he would have been job hunting that very afternoon.

The hours ticked by until five o'clock arrived, and I had no choice but to wrap up the email I'd been distractedly attempting to write and shut my computer down. I heard trash cans being moved out from under desks, so the cleaning crew that came in several evenings a week would not forget to empty them. I heard Kristy telling Bryce to have a good weekend. The Friday workday had officially ended.

Kristy appeared in my doorway, briefcase slung over one shoulder and a lunch bag in her hand. "I know we've been teasing you more than usual this week. I'm glad you're a good sport." She came in and enveloped me in a big bear hug. "Have a great time tonight," she said.

"I'm sure I will," I lied. "Thanks."

She left the office, and a few seconds later, I heard the front door of the studio clunk closed.

I gathered up the few papers I needed to take home with me and placed them in my briefcase. I looked up as Bryce stopped in the doorway, grinning.

"Okay, boss, knock 'er dead tonight!"

A sudden nervousness bubbled up, and it must have shown on my face because he moved closer. "It'll be fine, don't worry."

I sat on the edge of my desk, arms crossed. "What makes you think I'm worried?"

"I may not have known you as long as Laurel has, but I know you nevertheless. You want everyone to think you're tough and self-sufficient, and you are to an extent, but part of you is all soft and fluffy, and despite all of your success, you're somewhat insecure. Besides, you've been on another planet all week. It's normal to be nervous."

"You know, I haven't gone out with anyone officially in a long time, not since before I moved here." I leaned back and propped myself on the edge of the desk as I studied his face. "I've gone out now and then, but nothing I would consider a date date, you know?"

Bryce nodded.

"My last relationship was a disaster. Really, that's the only word that can be used to describe it. Laurel wasn't exaggerating at all when she mentioned Julie. Being with her was just…just awful, and it could have ended up very badly. I don't know if I'm ready to go through all that again." I sighed.

Bryce came over to me and rested a reassuring arm around my shoulders.

"What do you mean, 'not ready?' Not ready for what? Not ready to have a good time? Not ready to make a new friend, have a few drinks? No one said that this will be anything more than that. Believe me, I can count on one hand the times that a date turned into anything more." He smiled warmly, showing perfect teeth.

I looked into his handsome face and saw true affection in his expression. I wondered for the hundredth time why this man was still single.

"Just go out there and loosen up. If she's that bad, which I doubt from the way Laurel has been selling her, then just get through it. Whatever happens, you'll live through the night."

I smiled and got up from my perch on the desk. I had to leave soon. "You make it sound so easy."

"What's so hard about dinner? You have to eat, right? Worst case, take her home and bang her brains out. At least you'll both get something out of the evening." He flashed another smile.

Caught off guard, I sputtered and coughed.

He laughed. "Loosen up. That was supposed to make you laugh."

"Ha ha. Happy now?"

"That's better. Now I have to get going. I have a date of my own."

My mouth formed an O. "Why didn't you tell me?" I asked,

incredulous.

"What? And have to tolerate the snide remarks and teasing like you did all week? No thanks."

I wadded up a sheet of paper from my desk and flung it at him. "Sneak!"

He chuckled and scampered from the room. "Don't forget movie night tomorrow," he called back, referring to the one night a month we all met to watch rented movies and order carry-out. "And I'll expect details. If I don't get them from you, I'll get them from Laurel." His voice faded as he moved toward the exit, and then I heard the bang of the door.

I gathered the last of my things and made sure the coffeemaker and toaster oven were turned off. Within a few minutes, I followed Bryce out the door. Normally I would have stayed later at the office, reviewing the week and preparing for Monday, but as everyone in the entire free world seemed to be aware, I had a date, and little more than an hour and a half to prepare for it.

Chapter Five

After inspecting my bedside clock for what had to be the tenth time since I'd left work, my nerves became more frazzled and I was instantly sorry I had checked at all. I was almost finished getting dressed, but my hair was still wet and I needed to redo my eye makeup.

I gathered up my shoes and slid them onto my tired feet, reminding myself to never again agree to anything like this after a full day at the office. I wanted to kick myself for leaving the office so late and allowing myself so little time to get ready. "I'm the boss. I can leave early once in a while. Why didn't I do that tonight?" I often spoke out loud to myself when stressed.

I rushed into the bathroom and worked some product into my hair, scanning myself in the mirror as I massaged the goo over my head. A quick glance at my dress confirmed that the deep purple was the right choice.

I grabbed the hair dryer and tossed my hair, trying to dry it quickly. Just styling my thick hair would take twenty minutes, and I surely didn't want to show up with damp hair. "Why did I waste so much time when I came home? I had plenty of time, but then I had to check email and listen to phone messages. Oh my God, Laurel is going to *kill* me if I'm late."

After putting the finishing touches on my hair, I dabbed some perfume on my wrists and started on my makeup with jittery hands. I took a deep breath to release the building tension as I hustled back to the bedroom and gave myself the once-over in the full length mirror. Even with a critical eye, I decided I looked good, or at the very least, good enough. My dress wasn't wrinkled, and I had matching shoes on. I was batting a thousand.

Foregoing a coat because of the warm spring temperature, I rushed out the door and hurried to my car. Considering the amount of time it had taken to style my hair, I decided against putting the top down on the car. I had only driven a short way toward the restaurant when I noticed the lever on the gas gauge hovering on "E."

"Noooooo. Shit! Goddammitsonofabitch! Oh my God, Nooooooooooooo." I slammed my palm on the steering wheel, which sent a whole new stream of obscenities spewing from my mouth.

"Why tonight?" I cried, reaching for my cell phone to call Laurel to tell her I'd be late, only to realize I'd left it behind in my rush to leave my apartment. "Shit!"

I considered my options and realized I'd be even later than I already was if I ran out of gas. I chewed the inside of my cheek and tried to remember the closest gas station on my route.

"Okay, there's one on Patrick. I should be able to make it that far. Dammit. I hope this isn't an omen that I should have stayed home."

A few miles later, I pulled into the station on fumes and

found every island full. I resigned myself to the fact that I would just have to choose the shortest line, which was already two cars long. I positioned my Jaguar behind a gaudy muscle car, hoping the driver would finish filling his car quickly.

While Mr. Muscle Car pumped the gas, I dug frantically into my purse, wanting to have my credit card handy the second he finished. Card in hand, I looked up to find another driver chatting with him and admiring his hotrod. Frustrated, I began rubbing my brow, feeling a headache beginning and trying to keep it at bay. "Just don't rub your eyes, Beth. All you need is to show up on this date smelling of gas, looking like you did your hair in a blender, and resembling a raccoon." I glanced again at Mr. Muscle Car. He was watching me talk to myself. Great.

Finally he reseated the hose, slowly eased into his car, and left with a great roar. I was sure that the loudness of the motor was to help convince him that a certain appendage was larger than it really was.

Desperate to fill the tank and get back on the road, I swerved around a car and pulled into the space in front of it. I gingerly climbed from the car, careful to not muss my dress. I went to the pump and swiped my credit card, then waited for confirmation that I could begin filling.

BEEP! The loud shriek made me jump. I squinted at the display and followed its insistence that I swipe the card again. BEEP! I was already on edge, and the second alert was more annoying than alarming. After the failed attempt, I stomped toward the mini-mart that housed the station. I was probably already late and close to hyperventilating. I glanced at my wrist and realized my watch sat on the dresser where I'd flung it earlier. *Maybe I should buy something, so they'll give me a bag to breathe into. Maybe if I'm really lucky, it'll be a plastic bag and I'll asphyxiate.*

I waited in a line of potato chip- and soda-buying patrons, tapping my credit card impatiently against my palm, which was sweaty from nerves. At last, I was at the counter, where a greasy-haired teenager watched me through half-lidded eyes. Great. I'd just walked into *Fast Times at Ridgemont High*.

"My credit card's not working at pump number eight," I explained, trying to stay calm.

"Uh, yeah. Did you try another pump?" he asked, clearly not interested.

"No, I didn't, mainly because I don't have time to move to another line and wait. There were two cars in front of me, and those drivers had no problems with the pump. Can you just run my card through or something?"

Without a word, the greasy teen grabbed the check card from my hand and turned toward the card scanner. I waited, tapping my foot, hoping against hope for a speedy transaction. Teenage boy finally turned back and said, "Yeah, your card isn't going through. Do you have another one?"

My mouth opened as I considered that. I did have other cards, but they were in the car, which would involve walking back out to the pump, getting the card, and coming back in, only to stand in the line that was quickly forming behind me.

"No, I don't," I lied. "Can't you run it through manually or something?"

He began shaking his head before the sentence was completely out of my mouth. "No can do. Sorry." He tilted his head lazily to the right. "We have an ATM, if you want to pay with cash," he offered as he handed me the card.

Oh my God! I looked around me, hoping to see some sympathetic looks, but only found the faces of people who wanted me to get out of the way so they could pay for their snacks and cigarettes. Without other options, I headed toward the ATM and quickly withdrew some cash, grateful that the card worked in that machine. I glanced at the clock hanging on the wall behind the cashier before moving back to the line to wait behind the three people ahead of me at the register.

I threw ten dollars at the cashier and hurried back to my car as quickly as my heels allowed.

"All right, come on, you. Pump like your life depends on it."

Giddy with relief when the pump shut off at the ten dollar mark, I replaced the cap and dove behind the wheel, then wove out of the parking lot as quickly as I could safely manage. It wasn't until I was back on the road that I realized I should have looked for a pay phone at the station. Although they were now few and far between, chances were there had been one. I was close to tears as I maneuvered the car from one lane to the next, knowing without a doubt that it was already well past seven, and wanting only to reduce the number of minutes I'd arrive late. I hoped that the three people waiting for me would forgive me, and that the city hadn't yet installed red light cameras on my route.

Chapter Six

It wasn't until I pulled my dusty blue Jaguar into the first available parking space inside the parking garage that I allowed myself a deep, calming breath. It didn't work. Even without my watch, I knew that I was very late, and that the instant Laurel spotted me, her eyebrows would arch into the position reserved for those times when she was angry with me. I wondered how many missed calls and voicemails I would find when my cell phone and I were reunited. I grabbed my purse, and, with my stomach in a tight knot, hurried toward the restaurant, wondering why I had ever quit smoking. I rubbed my jaw, which was sore from clenching.

I raced down three flights of stairs and walked as quickly as I could to the restaurant, careful not to break an ankle. Why had I let Laurel talk me into wearing these shoes? Out of breath and starting to sweat, I entered the restaurant and was immediately greeted by the smiling host.

"I'm meeting some people at seven. I'm late, obviously," I stammered, hoping he could make sense of my gibberish. "The reservation is under Stevens," I guessed, hoping that Laurel would have made the reservations under her own name.

"Yes, they've been waiting," he informed me. "Follow me, please." His calmness did nothing to ease the tension that was tying my stomach in knots.

I located Laurel at a table around the corner.

She was staring in my direction, blankly. If I knew her at all, which I did, she'd been staring at this entrance from the second she sat down. Upon seeing me, she smiled, relief written across her face, and she waved as two heads turned in my direction. Will waved also, but he was just a blur in my peripheral vision.

My gaze was riveted on my date for the evening, who was watching me with a slight smile. Had Laurel described her to me, the details would have fallen short of the reality. Dark hair cascaded over her shoulders. Her face was slender, accentuated with high cheekbones made even more prominent by a touch of color, and even before I reached the table, I was struck by deep, dark eyes which were a chocolaty brown. My breath caught in my throat, and I instantly forgave Laurel for arranging this meeting as I rushed forward to be introduced. Laurel had not been kidding when she said she'd found me a lesbian. Boy, had she ever.

"Do you know how late you are?" Laurel squawked. "I thought you weren't coming."

"Yes, I do. I'm sorry." I turned to my date and repeated, "I'm so sorry."

Toni smiled then, a great, gleaming smile that warmed me. Wow. The heat began in my cheeks and dripped down into my belly. The woman was gorgeous.

"It's all right. You have all evening to convince me that you have a valid excuse," she teased as she extended her hand toward me.

Ooooh, not timid. A definite turn on.

"I'm Toni Vincent." Her voice was as deep and honey-rich as I imagined it would be when I saw her face. It was a throaty rasp that did nothing to lower my body temperature.

I opened my mouth to respond, then closed it again to give myself time to ensure I hadn't said any of my thoughts out loud. "Beth Anders." I shook her hand as Will stood and held my chair for me.

"Glad you could make it," Will kidded as he settled back into his seat. "You can thank me later for keeping her calm," he murmured.

"Where's your cell phone?" Laurel asked, oblivious to everything except that I was late.

"This is calm?" I said to Will, then turned back to Laurel. "I'm sorry, Laurel. I rushed out of the house without it. My fuel tank was on empty. I...let's just say that everything that could have gone wrong did, okay?" I settled into my chair, vowing to not let the stress of getting to the restaurant late and my friend's potentially sour mood ruin my own evening.

Laurel was not going to let me off easy. "Because you left work too late."

I sighed. "Yes, because I left work too late. Forgive me." I turned to Toni and repeated the apology, but in a more heartfelt manner.

Toni was sipping her drink, not a foofy, girly drink, but a real drink. She held the small tumbler and watched me while she swirled the cubes around. She examined me with a slight grin upturning the left side of her mouth. It reminded me of the way

Laurel looked when she was trying to read my mind, but this was sexy. Very sexy.

If anything at all about this beautiful woman indicated what she was thinking, it was her bright crystal eyes. Expressive and glistening, they seemed to dance as she watched me. She had slight smile lines surrounding her eyes, and long, dark lashes. Her hair was dark and wavy, with honey highlights. She watched me as if she wanted to make sure she had my full attention before responding to my apology.

"Don't worry about it. It happens to us all," she offered, making me like her instantly. "I'm glad you're here." She tilted her glass toward me as if she was toasting my presence, and then she took a sip. She made even that action look sexy.

"So am I."

I glanced at Laurel, who had an annoying "I told you so" grin plastered on her know-it-all face. The way she was watching me, I could tell that she knew I liked what I saw. "I don't know if Laurel told you, but she has a sadistic streak," I commented.

"She also worries about you. That was evident before you got here," Toni said gently.

I was instantly sorry I'd made the dig. "I know she does, but it was just one of those days, believe me. I really am sorry. I'm not normally unreliable."

"I forgive you." Toni lightly touched my wrist, and then rested her chin on her hand. This woman had Flirting 101 down pat. She listened intently as I related the problems I'd encountered on my way to the restaurant.

We all laughed over the tale of the incompetent teenaged

cashier. A half hour earlier, I wouldn't have imagined that I'd be laughing about the situation.

Toni's eyes sparkled each time I looked at her, and I hadn't yet figured out if she was intentionally flirting with me, or if she was just naturally seductive. I was instantly smitten.

I ordered a glass of wine and leaned back in my chair, finally able to relax. I glanced across the table to where Laurel was smiling at me warmly. I returned the smile and received a wink in return. This was the Laurel I loved. I knew she was a control freak, and she enjoyed giving me a hard time, but she truly had a good heart, and she loved me.

I turned to Toni and caught her giving me a strange look, which was quickly replaced by a crooked smile.

Toni was quite a conversationalist, I found, as we talked about a wide range of topics. She would watch me intently as I spoke to her, often absently placing a wayward lock of hair behind her ear while she listened. I tried not to stare, but found her gestures almost hypnotic. Her lips, which outlined her perfect white teeth, caught my attention as she spoke, and I couldn't help imagining how it might feel to be kissed by her. *Whoa. Too soon. Way too soon to be thinking of that.*

Will and Laurel each held up their end of the conversation throughout the evening, and I was relieved to find that it was turning out to be a fun evening out. I was constantly turning my gaze to Toni. Each time I glanced at her, she met my eyes with an intent stare, and her smile alone was enough to ignite a fire deep inside me.

~ ~ ~

Dinner was lovely. The four of us spent several hours enjoying each other's company, but eventually Will announced that the babysitter's time was winding down.

Toni leaned toward me and whispered, "I'm not ready to call it a night, are you?"

I didn't know what she had in mind, but I was intrigued. I shook my head.

She nodded at Will and Laurel. "Let's ask them if they'd like to go somewhere else." We left the restaurant and formed a semi-circle out on the sidewalk in front of the restaurant.

"Are you sure you guys can't squeeze in a quick cup of coffee with us?" I asked.

Will shook his head. "We told the babysitter we'd be back by eleven."

His response left me selfishly happy at the thought of being alone with Toni. My guilt was quickly replaced with elation over having my chaperones call it a night. We agreed to walk back to the parking garage together so that Toni and I could take my car to a coffee shop that boasted evening entertainment along with tasty brews. There was relatively little conversation on the short walk to the car, though Toni did lean closer to tell me she loved my dress. That made the shopping hassle with Laurel well worth it.

Laurel stood with us while Will paid the parking fee.

I rubbed my arms against the slight chill in the spring air.

"Toni, you'll have to come over for dinner soon. The girls still talk about you playing the piano with them."

Toni laughed, a warm, throaty sound. "That was fun. I would love to do that again soon."

Laurel rubbed my arm. "Maybe we can have you both over. You guys should get going before this one turns into a popsicle."

Will waved his goodbye, noticeably worried that the babysitter would charge them overtime.

Laurel leaned in for a hug. "Behave yourself," she whispered in my ear. She hugged Toni, and then she hurried to the car with Will, their hands clasped.

I smiled at that. They didn't have enough couple time together.

Now alone with Toni, I became somewhat shy. "My car's up here." I motioned toward the stairs. I paid my fee, and we went up the stairway.

Toni showed the proper appreciation when she saw my car, moving her up a notch on my list of Most Liked People In The World. Anyone who appreciated my vintage Jaguar for the beauty it was immediately earned my respect.

"This is absolutely gorgeous," she said as she ran her finger across the side. "My dad had a 1965 Jag. I wanted to own it when I was old enough to drive, but he had sold it long before then."

Her pout made her absolutely adorable. My grin was a mile wide.

We drove with the windows open just enough to allow the sweet smell of spring into the car. The coffee shop was less than a mile away from the downtown area, and I easily found a parking space in the shop's small parking lot. Inside, the place was filled with loud Friday night revelers, high on caffeine and eager to hear some music.

Toni led me to a small corner table for two in the least boisterous area of the shop, and offered to place our order while I saved the table.

"Do you come here often?" I mentally slapped my head with the realization of how cliché my question sounded.

"An ex-girlfriend of mine worked here" she answered, confirming my suspicion. "Very gay-friendly. Have you been here before?"

"I have, but only to pop in for coffee and pop right back out. I usually hit Starbucks, since it's so close to my studio."

"I'll get us some coffee."

I wouldn't sleep for a week, but I didn't care. I watched Toni's perfect ass glide toward the coffee counter. Oh my. It had been a long time since I'd looked at anyone's ass, other than Laurel's.

Toni returned quickly, and we resumed the conversation we had begun in the restaurant. I was amazed at how easy it was to talk to Toni, and I chalked it up to her skills as a teacher.

"How did you become a designer?" she asked suddenly.

"Hmmm, well, in college, my main focus was fine art. I had no idea what I would do with a degree in Fine Arts, but then I met Laurel. She was a Graphic Arts major. I'm a bit of a capitalist, in that I had no interest in being a starving artist." I laughed. "Moving into advertising seemed like a no-brainer. I like being secure and knowing where my next meal is coming from."

"You must be good if you have your own studio."

"I'm lucky. I know what I'm doing, and I have a good staff," I answered. "What about you? Why teaching?"

She beamed. "It seemed a logical choice for an English major, I think. And I love kids. I actually never saw myself teaching at the level I'm at. I thought of myself more as an elementary school teacher, but this is the path my career took, for whatever reason. I'm still not ruling out eventually teaching younger kids, and I would love to have my own someday."

She looked at me as if to gauge my reaction to her statement, but I simply smiled and sipped my coffee. Was I being quizzed on a first date about whether I wanted kids? The thought made me a bit uncomfortable, and I hoped my instinct was wrong. I'd always loved kids and could easily see myself in the role of being a mom, but my parents had done so much damage to me emotionally, I wasn't sure I'd ever be ready for that big step.

Toni reached across the table and casually took my hand. I liked it very much. I had forgotten how good simple physical contact with another woman felt. We talked about books we'd read, places we'd visited, and it turned out we had quite a bit in common. We both ordered refills, not wanting the night to end.

~ ~ ~

It was almost two a.m., and I didn't have a clue as to how I would manage to fall asleep when I got home. The drive back to her car was short and quiet, but companionably so. My caffeine-fueled fingertips tapped out a rhythm on the wheel as I drove. I pulled my car in close to the entrance of the parking garage and shut off the engine.

Toni turned to me and took my hand. Her skin was warm and soft, and her hand fit into mine perfectly. In the light from the street lamps and the illuminated garage, I could see her face. She was smiling as I sat examining her face and admiring her absolute beauty.

"You're absolutely stunning." I gasped. *Oh my God, I actually said that out loud!*

An amused laugh bubbled up, and Toni covered her mouth. "You didn't mean to say that out loud, did you?"

I shook my head.

"I could tell. You should see your face right now."

I could feel the hot flush starting in my neck and moving up toward my cheeks.

"Don't be embarrassed. I think it's adorable, and thank you. I think you're a very beautiful woman too."

I ran my fingertips over my brow, hoping to remove any nervous perspiration before she could notice it.

"When Laurel asked me if I wanted to go out with a friend of hers, I never thought it would turn out this well," she confessed. "I almost said no. Well, I *did* say no...*tried* to say no, but Laurel's hard to turn down. I'm glad I didn't go with my first instinct this time."

I nodded. "I know exactly what you mean."

Toni leaned her head back against the headrest and watched me. Her eyes focused on my lips, and I read her intent in her eyes. It was too soon.

"I should get going," I said as I looked out the windshield at nothing in particular.

"Do you have any plans for tomorrow?"

I turned back to her, and the glint in her eyes told me she was hoping my schedule would be clear.

"You mean today?" I asked with a grin, noting the early hour on the clock on the dash.

"Yeah," she said, her voice breathy.

"Not yet."

She smiled widely. "Do you want to get together?"

"Yes." Yes was an understatement. I didn't want to leave her at all. I reached across her to open my glove compartment. I pulled a business card from a case, and handed it to Toni.

"My cell number is the second one," I said.

"I'll call you as soon as I get up," she promised, opening the car door. She ducked down to wish me goodnight, waved, then disappeared into the parking structure.

I sat alone for a minute, still feeling her with me. I could smell her light perfume, and it turned my insides to mush. My olfactory senses have always had a close relationship with my libido. There was nothing like a beautiful woman who smelled good. I drove the entire way home with a grin plastered on my face.

Chapter Seven

The cell phone shook me from my sleep. I'd been dreaming of walking down a long hotel corridor, and my sleepy brain thought the dinging sounds were coming from an elevator I had been ready to step inside. Sitting up, I considered throwing the phone against the wall before I recalled the previous evening and hoped the caller would be Toni.

"Hello?" I answered hopefully.

"I was sure you'd call me by now. How did last night go after we left?"

I groaned, regretting that I hadn't checked the Caller ID before answering. "Laurel?" I tried to shake the sleep from my brain. "What time is it?"

"Did I wake you up?" Before I could respond to her question, she went on. "Is Toni there with you?"

I rubbed at my eyes. "No, I'm alone. What kind of loose woman do you take me for?" I teased. "I had a great time last night, by the way, and I'll thank you properly when I'm fully awake." I looked at the clock next to my bed. *Definitely too early to be awake on a Saturday.*

"So it went well after we left?" Laurel prodded.

I knew she wouldn't leave me alone until I at least gave her some details.

"We went to a coffee shop and talked for a long time." I smiled at the memory of the previous night. "She's gorgeous, smart, she's...she's everything you said, you know?" I was suddenly shy, and finding it difficult to put my feelings into words.

"I'm impressed. You usually keep everyone at arm's length until they prove themselves to you. What did she do to convince you so quickly?"

Knowing she didn't expect an answer, I just laughed.

"I'm glad it went so well," she said seriously. "Come over for lunch, and you can tell me everything."

I almost agreed before remembering that I might have other plans.

"I can't. Toni said she'd call me today, and we'd do something together." I cringed, waiting for a complaint, a sigh, or some other sign of disappointment, but none came.

"Well, it must be love. You're snubbing your friends already," Laurel ribbed.

"I'm sorry."

"That's okay. I'm glad you like her. I knew you would. If I wasn't married, I'd date her."

I opened my mouth to respond to that, but was interrupted by a crashing sound on her end.

"No, you guys. Get down from there! Listen, Beth, I have to go. I'll talk to you later." Without another word, the call ended.

I crawled from my bed and opened the curtains in my room. The pollen coating my window tinted everything yellow, but I was warmed by the spring sunshine filtering through the glass. I made a mental note to have the windows washed, and was lost in my thoughts when the phone rang again.

"Hello?" I answered for the second time in minutes.

"Hi. Hope I didn't wake you."

Toni's smoky voice warmed me as much as the sunshine. The back of my neck tingled. I took a second to get my bearings, and wondered how someone I hadn't even known twenty-four hours could affect me so deeply.

"Hi," I breathed into the phone. "Laurel beat you to it, but just by a minute or two." I knew my smile could be heard in my voice. So much for playing it cool.

"Are you planning on sleeping in, or would you like to get out in this beautiful weather and have lunch with me?"

It sounded almost as if it was a dare. "Tell me where and when, and I'll be there."

Toni laughed and gave me directions to her apartment.

We hung up with plans to meet in a few hours. Today was going to be a beautiful day, and not just because of the weather.

~ ~ ~

I pulled my hair into a pony-tail before pulling away from the curb. I guided my car, top down, to the address Toni had given me. It was an attractive older house that had been converted into an apartment building. I could spend a lifetime on that front porch, with its fat, comfortable-looking chairs and porch swing. The neighborhood was a bustle of activity due to the sun-warmed weather and its proximity to a park, and it had a homey feel. I found a parking space on the street nearby, went inside the building, and located the flight of stairs Toni had said would lead me to her flat.

I ran my hands over my jeans, making sure they hadn't wrinkled on the short drive over, licked my middle fingertip and ran it over my eyebrows, and lifted my arms to make sure I didn't have any embarrassing sweat stains. "Okay, ready as I'll ever be, I guess."

I climbed the stairs, knocked at the first door, as instructed, and was greeted by Toni within seconds. She was wearing a simple t-shirt tucked into a pair of faded jeans, and looked as comfortable as she had in dress and heels the night before. And she was just as beautiful in natural daylight as she had been by lamplight. I knew right then that I was in trouble.

"Hi. Come on in, I'm almost ready." She led me into her cavernous living room, where sunlight was streaming in through large windows along two walls.

Toni's hair fell into place around her face as it had when we'd met, and in the sunlight, I noticed that the highlights in her hair were more prominent and they certainly were natural.

"Would you like a drink? I just made some iced tea."

My mouth was dry from the sight of her, and I barely squeaked, "Sure." I settled onto the sofa and took in my surroundings as she left the room. She had excellent taste in furnishings and could probably have tried her hand at interior design if she'd had the inclination. Although the exterior of the house had an aged appearance, Toni's apartment had a modern air. Light sages mixed with deep corals, reminding me of the southwest. As far as I could see, the entire place was roomy, bathed in sunlight, with rich colors which were reflected in the blonde hardwood floors.

Toni returned with two tall glasses of iced tea, handed me mine and sat down next to me.

"You look great," she offered, along with a smile that melted my insides.

I noticed a small cleft in her chin that I hadn't seen the night before. Her eyes sparkled as she smiled. She licked her lips, and my heart rate nudged up into another gear.

"I just need to get some shoes on, and then we can go."

I looked down and saw that she was indeed barefoot. She had delicate feet, and her nails were polished with a very feminine, sexy color.

She set her glass down on an end table and shot out of the room, returning almost instantly with a pair of leather sandals dangling from two fingers. She plopped onto the sofa next to me and slipped her feet into the sandals. I wondered if she always had so much energy. This dynamo would be hard to keep up with in many ways. My wicked mind was imagining the ways when she pushed a strand of my hair out of my eyes, ending my musings. Our eyes locked for a second before Toni glanced down at my lips. I braced myself for a kiss that didn't come.

"Any idea of where you want to go?" she asked, breaking the spell.

I shook my head to clear the daze she had me in. "I haven't even thought about it."

"Well, I'm sure we'll be able to agree on something. We seem to have a great deal in common."

Yeah, like being hopelessly in lust with each other.

She stood and tugged on my hand until I was standing beside her. "Ready?"

I nodded, and we were off.

~ ~ ~

We ended up ordering lunch from a nearby deli and then walking to the park near Toni's apartment. Lunch was a picnic on the delicate spring turf. Blades of grass poked us wherever they found exposed skin. Inches apart, we talked incessantly while we watched the people around us. Every now and then a breeze would rustle over us, and Toni would absently reach up to tuck her hair behind her ear. Such a simple move, and yet so sexy.

She squinted at me, her chin upturned.

"Something you need to see better?" I asked as I moved closer.

She flashed me a grin and moved her finger up to my forehead, where she rubbed a spot near my eyebrow. "What's this scar from? It's kind of sexy. Did you get it running from the bulls in Pamplona?" She smiled and bit her lip.

I removed her hand from my face and held it in my lap. "Uh, no. My last girlfriend gave it to me."

All signs of playfulness disappeared from her face. "Oh my gosh! Not intentionally, right? Please tell me she didn't do that to you on purpose."

My silence answered her.

"Oh, Beth, I am so sorry I joked about it. I thought you were going to say that one of Laurel's girls bonked you on the head with something or... I, I had no idea."

I squeezed her hand. "No, it's okay. You had no way of knowing. Don't feel bad about it."

Her eyes searched mine. "Do you want to talk about it?"

I shook my head. "It was a long time ago."

She looked so concerned, I hoped this hadn't ruined the mood. Bad memories of Julie tried to wriggle into my mind, but I pushed them away and smiled at Toni.

Her eyes sparkled with compassion. "What are you thinking about?"

I didn't know if I wanted to tell her. I took a deep breath and blew it out, then scanned my surroundings before I looked back at her. I tugged up some grass and brushed the blades across her hand. "I'm just happy. I'm having a good time with you, and I like you a lot." I scrunched my nose and looked away.

Laurel had been right. I usually kept people at a distance, because I didn't want to get hurt again. Toni had instantly pushed her way through that reticence, and I wasn't sure why that was.

"All right, let's lighten the mood then. How long have you had a crush on Laurel?" Her eyes, full of mischief, never left my face.

"What?" I sputtered, and looked away, unable to make eye

contact. "You're insane!"

Toni laughed, but it didn't sound condescending. "Come on, you can't fool me. I saw it right away at the restaurant. I saw the look you gave her."

If my blush had gotten any hotter, my face would have burned up in an instant. I was mortified. If Toni could read my emotions so easily after just meeting me, what had Laurel and Will seen on my face all these years?

Toni reached out and rubbed my knee. The warmth of her hand through the denim of my jeans was comforting, but I still couldn't look at her.

"Beth, don't be embarrassed. Geez, I've had a crush on her since I met her. How could I not? My God, she's gorgeous." Her hand moved to my shoulder. "But she has nothing on you."

I turned to face her. "I admit it flares up now and then, but only when Laurel is being nice."

Toni smiled warmly.

"Which is almost never," I added dryly.

Toni laughed, which dispelled any remaining tension.

"We've all been there, believe me," Toni assured me. "I feel as if I already know you well," she said, changing the subject. "Is that strange?" She was sitting cross-legged next to me, her finger unconsciously twirling a strand of her hair. She did that often, and I found the habit wildly sexy.

"Oh, I don't know," I answered playfully. "Tell me everything you know about me so far."

Toni sat up straighter, apparently taking my challenge seriously. She ticked items off on her fingers as she spoke.

"Hmm, okay well, you're...around my age, right?"

I nodded. Toni's age was one detail Laurel had shared with me.

"You drive a convertible," she continued, tapping her second finger. "A very cool convertible that would make my dad fall in love with you."

"Well, now you're cheating. You rode in my car, so that wasn't hard to figure out," I teased.

"Okay, I'll give you that one. Hmm, what else? All you've ever wanted to do with your life is to be an artist—"

"Nope."

"Nope? What did I miss?" She seemed to be enjoying the game.

"I wanted to do something besides design, but it was out of my reach." I frowned dramatically to underscore my feigned unhappiness.

"I can't imagine anything being out of your reach. What was it?"

I could tell she was amused. "Don't laugh," I implored.

She nodded solemnly.

"When I was in college, there was something I wanted desperately. I...I wanted to...marry Stevie Nicks. Honestly! Don't laugh, you promised."

Despite her vow, Toni was giggling helplessly. "You're not serious?" she said between spurts of laughter.

"Yes, I'm serious. I fell for her and decided that I would give up my career entirely if I had a chance with her. I still might, I don't know. Maybe she'd like my car too. "

"And this was unobtainable because she's famous, right?"

"Well yeah. It's sort of hard to date someone who doesn't know you exist. That, and the fact that she's straight, but that's a minor detail."

She wasn't just giggling anymore; she was now hysterically in stitches. She was laughing so hard, I couldn't help but join her.

"I'm sorry," she wheezed. "I know I promised not to laugh. You weren't serious, were you?"

"Not completely, so I forgive you." I eyed Toni playfully. "So, tell me, why did you need to see a photo of me before agreeing to go out with me?"

Toni leaned back on the grass, her bare elbows digging into the ground, and I pictured the indentations the grass was making in her skin.

"Desperate as it sounds, I agreed to the date sight-unseen," I teased.

She grinned and sat up, then leaned closer to me. A slight breeze drifted by, and I caught a whiff of her intoxicating perfume. *I need to ask her what that is, so I can buy some to spray on my pillowcase. Oh my yes, I have it bad.*

"Mmm, well it's not that I asked to see a photo. More like I kept saying 'no' to Laurel's offer to set us up until I saw a photo of you on their piano." She chuckled. "Once I saw you, there was no question that I wanted to go out with you."

I could feel the heat creeping up my neck.

"I don't like being set up. I've been through so many bad relationships, especially the last one, and I was kind of tired of trying to find someone."

Her bluntness was beginning to worry me. Was she trying to tell me there was no chance of us having a relationship? She seemed to read the uncertainty on my face, as she smiled and brushed a lock of hair away from my eyes.

"And then I saw the picture of you, and something happened. I'm not sure what it was — just a feeling that came over me. It didn't hurt that you're a very attractive woman, and that photo doesn't even do you justice. I wanted to meet you after that."

"Wow."

"Yeah, wow," she agreed. "And I haven't been at all disappointed."

We sat in companionable silence, watching the sunset, neither one of us wanting to leave the other.

I checked my watch. "Are you hungry?" It had been hours since we'd eaten the sandwiches, and my stomach was beginning to protest.

"Now that you mention it. What do you have in mind?"

"How about if we swing around to the supermarket and pick up a few things, and I'll make you dinner?"

~ ~ ~

I put two steaks under the broiler and joined Toni on my sofa.

"You've got a terrific place here," she commented

I'd always considered the house a bit gothic for anyone's

taste but mine. Laurel had always referred to it as the Bat Cave. High arches framed each doorway, and a sturdy wooden stairway led to the loft overlooking the living room which housed my bedroom.

"Thank you. This is a very old building, but I like the style."

She smiled as I handed her a glass of wine.

"You have a beautiful smile." *There I go again, spewing out everything that enters my mind.*

"Thank you, Beth. You're good for my ego. Do you always say everything you think?" She smiled again, softening the bluntness of her candor.

"Uhhh, not usually."

Toni set her drink on the coffee table. She turned to me, cradled my face in her hands, and kissed me softly.

My body responded instantly. I curled my fingers into her thick hair, playing gently with the dark locks. Her tongue nudged my lips, and I parted them, and met her tongue with mine. The desire between us was quickly becoming stronger. When Toni's arms wrapped around me, a deep sigh rose in my throat. It had been a long time since a woman had held me, but I couldn't recall any other ever making me feel this way.

I smelled smoke and suddenly remembered dinner. "The steaks! I have to check them. I'll be right back." I raced into the kitchen and switched on the light inside the oven. I could see that I was just in time. Another minute or two, and the meat would have been leather. Not that it mattered. My stomach was no longer the part of my body that was feeling hunger. I hurried back to the sofa, with no immediate interest in anything but

Toni.

Toni was sitting as I had left her. Her arm was resting on the back of the sofa, and her breathing sounded slightly labored. She watched me intently as I crossed the room to her.

"Dinner's ready."

She smiled. "I think I've lost my appetite. Are you hungry?"

My heart did not want to move so quickly. Things were proceeding way too fast, but other parts of my body did not want to hear the concerns of my heart. "No. Last thing on my mind." Sitting beside her, I pulled her close and resumed our kiss.

She rested her hands on my sides and her fingers tentatively stroked up and down. After pulling my shirt from my jeans, she slid her hands underneath, eliciting a sharp intake of air from me. The skin on skin contact was making the room swirl. Her kisses became deeper and more urgent. Her hand cupped my breast, and another moan of pleasure escaped me.

My thoughts swirled as my body relaxed and welcomed Toni's touch. It had been so long since I'd experienced physical affection, the feel of Toni's hands on me triggered a host of feelings. The few encounters I'd had over the years had been heavy on desire and low on emotion. Now I was finding that her caresses were so freeing, I wondered briefly why I had fought this possibility for so long. I hoped we'd be heading upstairs to my bed before too long.

And then the doorbell rang.

We pulled ourselves apart and looked at each other miserably.

"Who is that?" I whispered breathlessly, not even thinking about how silly it was for me to be asking her who was at my door.

Frowning, Toni shrugged. I could see she didn't welcome the intrusion any more than I did.

The bell rang again, followed by a sharp knock.

"You'd better get it."

Toni tagging along behind me, I moved toward the door, all the while hoping that by the time I reached it, the unwanted visitor would have given up and gone away. I opened the door slowly, wishing for a miracle. There stood my closest friends, the people I loved most in the world, the people I least wanted to see right at that moment.

My mouth dropped open.

It wasn't hard for them to figure out what had been happening inside my apartment. My shirt was wrinkled and untucked from my jeans, my hair, mussed. Toni's appearance was almost identical.

"Hi," Laurel said brightly. "Oh! This is a bad time, isn't it?"

She stood inches away from the door, both her girls in tow. Will stood beside them, and Bryce peeked over their shoulders with an unfamiliar man close by. Toni linked her fingers linked through my belt loop and smiled at the crowd.

"I'm sorry, we'll leave," Laurel offered.

I was trying to decipher why they were all standing at my door, when I realized they were waiting to come in. "No! Uh, no, don't leave. I'm sorry, I'm being rude. Come in." I moved aside and opened the door, my eyes sending Toni an apology for the disruption.

My friends filed in and gathered in the living room.

I pretended to scratch my head in order to try and tamp down my hair. Judging by how Toni's looked, it probably was quite mussed . "Uh, what are you all doing here?"

"Movie night, remember?"

I turned toward Bryce, then glanced at the stranger alongside him and tilted my head.

Catching my hint, Bryce introduced me. "This is Kenny, my date from last night," he reminded me. "And this must be yours." He nodded toward Toni, hand outstretched.

She shook it as I introduced them.

"Look, it's pretty obvious you forgot about tonight, and you have other plans, so why don't we make it another night?" Will suggested.

Each of the girls was hanging on a leg as they looked up at me, smiling.

"Hi, sweeties." I patted Becca on the back. "No, it just slipped my mind, but it's fine, isn't it?" I looked at Toni, who was already helping Kira remove her jacket.

"Absolutely," Toni responded. "We were just discussing renting a movie, so this is perfect." *Good save. Where has this woman been all my life?*

None of our guests looked convinced, but I settled them in the living room. I excused myself to pour drinks, and pulled Toni with me into the kitchen.

"I'm so sorry, I forgot. We get together once a month to watch videos and have food delivered, and it's my turn to host. I forgot all about it. If I had remembered, I could have canceled, but—"

"It's all right," she soothed, stroking my hair.

"I could take you home if you don't want to stay," I offered.

"Do you want me to stay?"

"I sure do. I like being with you, and getting to know you, and I... Yes, I want you to stay."

She smiled broadly and kissed me. "I'll stay as long as you want me to."

I could feel the warmth of her lips heating me from the outside in. I vaguely heard someone walk into the room and cough demonstratively.

"I never would have guessed that you two would be getting along so well this quickly."

I pulled away from Toni and turned to face Laurel. She had her "I told you so" grin plastered on her face.

"So, you're glad you took me up on my offer, aren't you?" She was addressing me, but I could see that Toni was smiling and nodding.

"Yes, I'm very glad," I answered reluctantly, not wanting to feed the inferno of her ego.

"Look, I just wanted to say that I had no idea we'd be interrupting anything. It's pretty obvious that you forgot we were coming over. Maybe we should do this another time," she suggested, reminding me again why she was my dearest friend. "Even though I did tell you earlier that I'd see you later."

I was tempted to accept her offer, but didn't have it in me to tell them all to leave. I was also conscious of the fact that Toni had promised to stay.

"No, it's fine. We want you to stay. Help me get drinks for everyone."

Toni and Laurel busied themselves with filling glasses with ice while I took orders for drinks in the living room and put in a call for pizza.

After I replaced the phone in its cradle, Bryce pulled me down beside him on the sofa. "Are you in love yet?" he asked.

"Well, Bryce, it's a little early for that, but let's just say that I'm closer than I've been in a very long time."

~ ~ ~

An evening spent hanging out with my friends had seldom been more fun. It was Bryce's turn to choose the movie, and he had picked *Miss Congeniality*, acting out random beauty pageant scenes throughout. We were in stitches at his antics, and I wasn't sure Toni would recover when Bryce imitated the snorting laughter of Sandra Bullock's character.

Laurel and Will's girls settled down on a blanket on the floor to enjoy their late night out at Aunt Beth's house. Both were sound asleep by 8:30. I noticed Toni watching them fondly and nudged her with my elbow so I could smile my appreciation. Anyone who loved those kids like I did got an A+ in my book.

I rose from the sofa, stacked plates and utensils, and then carried them to the kitchen and placed them in the dishwasher.

Toni followed me. She rested her hand on my lower back as I bent to line the plates up.

"Let me help. What can I do?"

I straightened and turned toward her. "Oooh, a woman who offers to help in the kitchen. You are quite the catch, aren't you, Toni Vincent?" I arched an eyebrow.

Her smile was luminous. "Yes. I am a great catch, Beth Anders. Kudos to you for figuring that out so quickly. You get extra points for noticing."

We laughed, and I pulled her into a hug. Her skin felt so good against mine. The passion flared, and, mindful of the guests in the living room, I pulled back and slung an arm around her shoulder. "Are you having a good time?"

She nodded. "Yes, ma'am, I am. I love hanging out with Laurel and Will, and your friends are hilarious. Plus, I get to spend time with you. Bonus." She brushed a quick kiss on my lips.

"Good, I'm glad." I rubbed my thumb along her shoulder, choosing my next words carefully. "I uh, I like you a lot, and I would really like it if we could start spending time together." She pursed her lips and nodded. "Please don't take this the wrong way, but I really need to move slowly. I...what happened earlier in there," I tilted my head toward the living room, "it was very nice, but I haven't been with anyone in a really long time, and I need to uh..."

Toni touched the puckered spot on my forehead. "This is about the scar?"

I nodded, watching her eyes for any signs that she was unhappy or disappointed with my request. There were none.

"You need to protect your heart, is what you're trying to say?"

I blew out a breath. "Yes. I didn't know that's what I was trying to say, but yes. Are you okay with that?"

She moved her palm to my cheek, and her eyes bored into mine. "Absolutely. I'm not looking for some quick roll in the hay. I like you, and I would like to see where this might lead. I'm a very patient woman."

There was that one-sided grin again. Taking it slow was not going to be easy.

"And I don't need to know what happened to you, but if and when you're ready to talk about it, I'm here, okay?"

I pressed my face against her palm. "Yeah, sure. I just didn't want to bring the mood down earlier because we were having such a nice time. We can talk whenever you want." I kissed her then, lingering just a moment so she could feel what I was trying to convey.

"Oh, for Pete's sake, you two. Seriously?" Laurel chided. "You met yesterday, and you can't keep your lips off each other?"

I felt Toni's lips turn up into a smile before the kiss ended. She turned toward Laurel and wrapped her arm around my waist. "Get used to it. I think you're going to be seeing a lot of it."

Chapter Eight

For the first time in a very long time, I felt that my life had purpose outside of work. The thought made me happy. The weekend had changed my life. Toni and I spent the entire day together on Sunday. By the time I drove home on Sunday night, I could scarcely bear to let her out of my sight.

Monday morning came, and for the first time in many years, work was not the first thing I thought of when I woke. The alarm jolted me awake, and I rubbed at my eyes, which felt as if they'd been pasted shut. After a few minutes, I sat up and swung my feet over the side of the bed and rubbed my bare feet back and forth across the rug, trying to motivate myself to get up and go to work. I walked to the dresser and checked my calendar on my phone. I could afford to be a little late today. *I wonder how early I can call Toni without being considered a stalker.*

By the time I shuffled into the office a half hour later than usual, I was carrying my second cup of coffee of the day, and a genuinely happy smile refused to leave my face. I found Bryce in the kitchen, whistling while he brewed a pot of coffee. I put my lunch in the fridge and then leaned against the counter, sipping my coffee.

"She's lovely," he said, a grin lightening his tired face as he scooped dark roast and deposited it in the coffeepot.

"Yes, she is," I agreed wholeheartedly. My beaming smile morphed into a shy grin. "Bryce, I'm surprised. I expected some crudeness from you this morning."

He smirked and rested a hand on my arm. "Oh, honey, there's plenty of time for that. I just thought I'd leave you to your afterglow until you're awake enough to fight back."

I playfully shoved his arm, and together we watched the coffee slowly drip into the pot.

"You care about her already, don't you?"

I nodded. "Yes, I do. I miss her, even though I was with her only…" I checked my watch, "…well, less than twelve hours ago. I think…I think I'm on my way to falling in love with her, and the funny thing is, for the first time in ages, it doesn't scare me at all. I've had the best weekend, you know?"

Bryce nodded.

"How did your weekend with Kenny go?"

"Well, I suppose not as well as yours, but Kenny and I will be seeing each other again."

When Kristy walked into the studio, she immediately demanded that I share the events of the weekend, since she hadn't been able to make our monthly movie social.

~ ~ ~

The day stretched out like a piece of chewing gum stuck between a shoe and a hot sidewalk. I missed Toni. I found myself daydreaming during slow moments of the day. I longed to hold her close. Butterflies fluttered in my stomach as I thought about her perfume, the way her hair felt between my fingers, how her eyelashes brushed against my face when she kissed my neck. Despite the elation I'd been feeling, there were many uncertainties swimming around my brain. After all these years alone, why was I suddenly so willing to be in a relationship? Did Toni want the same things I did? We'd left each other with no plans to meet again anytime soon. Could I trust Toni to not break my heart the way Julie had? I had known Toni for less than three days, and yet I was ready to throw a rope around her and hitch my future to hers.

By three o'clock, my mind and stomach were both filled with acid. The phone in my office rang, and I saw by the number on the Caller ID that it was Laurel calling.

"I was wondering how long it would take you to call me up for an interrogation. Honestly, Laurel, I don't know how you made it this long," I said by way of greeting.

"You're not the only one I can get the scoop from, you know, so don't play coy with me," she replied.

"You talked to Toni?" My pulse quickened. Butterflies fluttered. Just the thought that talking to Laurel now created a connection to Toni made me warm and cold at once.

"Of course I did. I work with her, remember?"

Curiosity got the better of me. "What did she tell you?"

"I wouldn't know where to begin. All she did all day was talk about you." That brought an immediate smile to my face, and many of the doubts I'd been feeling all day drained away. "She thanked me for introducing her to you and said that you two spent the entire weekend together. I figured I would wait to get the more graphic details from you."

I heard Toni's already familiar laugh, deep and throaty and extremely sexy, in the background as Laurel took a deep breath.

"She's standing right here. Do you want to talk to her?"

I could hear the smile in her voice. "Yes!"

I heard shuffling as Laurel apparently handed her cell phone to Toni, then Toni was on the line, her rich, sweet voice purring in my ear as it had the previous night.

"Hi, Beth. How are you?"

How can just a voice make me feel so many things? "I'm fine, except that I miss you terribly."

She chuckled. "Good. I'm glad I'm not the only one."

The words made my heart glow.

"Listen, I know we didn't discuss any plans for during the week, but how about if I repay you for dinner tonight? I need to talk to you about something."

Worry crept into my chest like warm liquid. I didn't hear anything unusual in her voice, but the invitation seemed ominous.

"Everything okay?" I asked, knowing that the worry I felt was evident in my voice but unable to prevent it.

"Yes, yeah, of course. Everything's fine. I just..." I heard her take a deep breath. "Things are happening really quickly, and there needs to be some ground rules for us. I don't mean to sound so dramatic, because I want to continue seeing you, but I need to let you know where I'm coming from before we move any further. Does that make sense?"

It didn't sound like she was ending what had started so quickly, but I wasn't sure what her ground rules would be. Toni hadn't given any indication the night before that she thought we were moving too quickly.

"Beth? Maybe I shouldn't have said anything, because now I've worried you, and what I want to talk to you about is no reason for you to get upset. I just really need to share some things with you tonight."

I breathed a small sigh of relief. Someone who planned on breaking up with you didn't go to that much trouble to put your fears to rest.

"Okay," I responded. "As long as everything's okay between us, sure, I'll be there after work."

"Good."

I could tell she was smiling, and that eased my worry even more. "I can't wait to see you." We made plans to meet at Toni's place at six.

When I set the phone onto its base, I was more at ease than I'd been all day, despite the fact that she wanted to have a serious discussion with me tonight.

Was it possible to be addicted to the sound of someone's voice, I wondered. I was feeling as if this love thing was something new the world had just begun to offer. Even though I didn't have anything to compare it to, I had the distinct feeling that this was different than anything I'd experienced before, that my past relationships couldn't have been love, or at least not love like this.

I felt a flutter deep inside. *Love. I just admitted I love her. Oh dear God, help me.*

~ ~ ~

Toni met me at her front door with a smile and a glass of wine.

My kind of woman. My smile stretched so wide, my face began to hurt. The concern that I wouldn't like what she wanted to discuss had been niggling at my brain all day, so this reception eased my mind.

"Come on in," she said. "I've got dinner started."

When I was inside, she smiled again and kissed me. She really does smile all the time, I thought as I returned her kiss and added a hug.

"Let's go into the kitchen so I can keep an eye on things." She took my hand and raised an eyebrow, giving me the welcome impression that dinner wasn't the only thing she wanted to keep an eye on.

I'd gone home first to change into casual clothes, and I was glad. She was wearing a pair of cargo shorts and was barefoot, making her just a hair shorter than I was in my sandals. She sat with me at the small table set off to the side of the small kitchen. Her glass of wine was waiting for her on the table.

I wanted to get the potentially awkward part of the evening out of the way. "So, you wanted to talk." I sipped my wine, barely registering the taste of it.

She reached over and touched my forehead. "Did I cause you anxiety about this? You carry your worries right here." She softly rubbed her finger along the lines on my forehead.

I took her hand and kissed her fingers.

She held my hand and rested her chin in her other hand, just watching me.

My heart sank into my stomach. I did not want what we had started to end. "What is it, Toni? Just tell me."

She sighed and tucked her hair behind her ear, her gaze never leaving me. "I just want to tell you where I'm coming from, and make sure we're on the same page."

"Okay."

"I just, well, a week ago I agreed to this very casual blind date, and now things have changed. So much. They've changed so much."

The acid that had been building in my stomach all day was bubbling up, scalding me with its presence. This conversation did not sound like it was going in the direction I had hoped. I gulped some wine and turned back to Toni, though it was difficult to meet her gaze.

"I'm not saying that the changes are bad. I'm not saying that I don't want this," she waved her hand between us, "to be serious. It's just been a huge surprise to me how I'm affected by you."

"Affected by me? What am I, a virus?" I snickered awkwardly at my failed attempt to lighten the mood and make myself feel better.

She smiled and cupped my face. "Oh my God, you are so adorable."

Finally, something that made me feel better about this

conversation.

"We've only known each other for a very short time, but I already feel as if I can see where this is going. Do you get what I'm saying?"

I nodded my head. I sincerely hoped she was feeling the same things I was.

"I have feelings for you, strong feelings, and I see us moving in the right direction, but..." She stopped to sip her wine, and I wasn't following what she was trying to tell me. She seemed so serious, but she had no intention of ending things, did she?

My heart raced, and I realized I was clenching my jaw. "Toni, please just tell me. Whatever it is, I will be fine. I can handle it."

When she smiled this time, the corners of her mouth barely moved upward. "I'm a little scared, Beth. I just want to make sure we're not those people who have a moving truck ready to go within a month of meeting each other. We agreed we'd move slowly, and I need that. And if we do decide we want to continue to see each other, I need you to be all in. I've already been with someone who was unfaithful and I can't...won't go through that again."

"I can do slow." I was relieved that this was what had been on her mind all day. "I could never be unfaithful. It's just not in me. I know how it feels to be betrayed, and I would never be the cause of such pain."

"I just needed to make sure we're on the same page, you know? My last relationship was a mess, and it ended very badly. For a long time, I really didn't think I would ever do this again."

Part of me wanted to maim the offender, but the other part

was happy that the woman had been dumb enough to lose Toni so I could have my chance. But I did want to know who had hurt her so badly, and how.

"What happened?"

Toni went to check on something on the stove, not saying a word until she returned to the table and settled back into her chair beside me.

"Um, she cheated. A lot. It was actually going on from very early in the relationship, but I didn't know about it until a month and a half before we broke up. I caught her with someone in our bed. She promised it wouldn't happen again, but a month later, I found out she was still seeing the woman I'd caught her with. I found out from friends afterwards that she had been sleeping with lots of people for a long time. People," she emphasized. "Guys, too, not just women. It crushed me."

She took a long sip of wine. When she looked at me, I could tell she was hoping I would understand her need to slow down. I did.

"Hey, it's okay. I'm so sorry that happened to you, but she's not me. I would never hurt you. Like I told you the other night, I need to take this one step at a time, too, so we can go as slowly as we both need, I promise."

Her face registered her relief.

"I don't know if Julie cheated on me, but I wouldn't be surprised to hear that she had. She drank a lot, and she was mean when she drank. I could never act that way to anyone I care about."

I hoped that she would believe me. It baffled me that people could be so cruel to those they professed to love.

She pursed her lips, and then broke into a wide grin. "I'm glad I found you." She moved her chair closer to mine and pulled me into her arms. "I've got to finish making dinner now, or we'll be eating burnt food."

Her lips turned up in a lopsided grin, and the knot in my stomach unwound. The issue was settled.

~ ~ ~

Weeks later, Toni and I sat sprawled on her soft leather sofa. We had rented a romantic comedy, but weren't giving the film much attention. My thigh lay across hers, and our heads rested close together on the back of the sofa. My hand rested on her bare thigh, just below the hem of her shorts, and occasionally snuck under her t-shirt to play with the smooth skin of her stomach. We talked until our hungry gazes moved us together, lips meeting, slowly at first, and then in a frenzy. I pulled back. Taking this relationship slowly would be the death of me. We had spent the last few weeks like this — spending time together talking, then getting closer and closer to the point of no turning back with the physical part of our relationship.

Toni smiled sympathetically. Her half-lidded eyes told me that she was as aroused as I was by our latest grappling session.

My breathing was ragged as I slowly twirled my finger across her stomach, distractedly making circles on her skin. I was lost in my own thoughts when she cleared her throat.

"Can I ask you something?"

Her voice sounded thick, like she had just woken up. I grinned, knowing my kisses had done that to her.

"Yeah, of course you can." *God, she's beautiful.* My insides turned to warm honey as I looked at her. Her face was free of cosmetics, and she was just as beautiful, if not more so, than the night we met. *Yeah, you're in love for sure.*

"You haven't told me much about your family," she said hesitantly.

The warm, wonderfully warm feeling drained away at the mention of my family. Ever since Toni had detailed her family life to me the night in the coffee shop, I'd been waiting for her to bring up that particular topic. Disbelief had washed through me as she described how she had come out to her parents when she was seventeen, and they had accepted her completely.

"Hey." She gently poked my bicep. "Are you still here? You went somewhere else just then." Her brow furrowed, and an adorable indentation appeared between her eyebrows.

Okay, maybe not *all* of the warm oozy feeling had left me.

"If you'd rather not talk about it, I understand."

But I could tell that she didn't understand. Having a close, supportive family, she couldn't even imagine how my upbringing was.

"Ermmm, no, it's fine. I don't want to keep anything from you." I trusted her enough to share the painful memories my parents had foisted on me. "What do you want to know?" My mood had changed, and I could hear the distress in my voice.

"Whatever you feel comfortable telling me, as much or as

little as you want." She angled herself so that she was facing me, and she stroked my hair as she spoke. "We don't have to talk about this at all, if you don't want to. I can tell I've upset you."

"No, it's okay. I don't like talking about it, but I want you to know. I need you to know everything about me." I rubbed my face and pondered where to begin.

I clasped my hands in my lap and focused on them. "I didn't admit to myself that I was a lesbian until my freshman year in college, not too long after I met Laurel," I began. "I had these feelings…for girls…way before then, but I think I probably knew how my parents would react to having a lesbian daughter, so I just repressed my longings and desires."

I stole a look at Toni. I had her complete attention.

"Until college, which is when I realized those feelings couldn't be buried anymore."

Toni nodded. Nearly every lesbian had a similar story.

"So, I met someone, and I fell hard and fast. I was so blinded by my elation that I decided to come out to my parents. I thought they'd be just as happy for me as I was for myself."

Toni sighed, likely seeing where my story was headed.

"Laurel had met my parents, and she tried to warn me." To my surprise, my fingernails were digging into my palms as I remembered my painful experiences. I'd thought I'd long since gotten past its impact.

"I told Laurel that I was planning to tell my parents, and she sat me down and gave me a talking to. She warned me that they might even put a stop to their financial support. That scared me." I sighed, and my lips trembled.. "They would have, too. Laurel made me swear that I would wait until after I graduated to tell them I was a lesbian ."

Toni placed a hand on my arm, and I felt her understanding and support. It had been years since I'd last told this horror story to anyone, and it was the first time in a while that I'd cried while reliving what had happened.

I swiped at the tears. "I didn't think this could upset me so anymore."

"It's okay, sweetie. Let it out."

"I had this weight hanging over me the entire time I was finishing school. I hated keeping such an important part of me a secret, but I had promised Laurel. When I would go home, I started noticing little comments and behaviors that indicated that they were homophobic. And not just homophobic. My parents were snobs. I always knew that they felt they were better than everyone else, but my senior year, I really started taking notice of their attitudes toward other people." I leaned against the back of the sofa and crossed my arms.

"I moved back home after graduation, and I made the colossal mistake of coming out to them my first week out of school." I drew a few ragged breaths. "They threw me out, told me they never wanted to see me again."

"Oh, Beth, I'm so sorry," Toni whispered.

"To be precisely accurate, my father refused to say anything as my mother threw me out. She said that I was a lesbian because I went to a liberal arts school and not a 'good' school, meaning one of the Catholic universities she had wanted me to attend. Then she told me that if she'd known that school would turn me into a pervert, she would never have paid my way, which confirmed Laurel's suspicions. They barely let me pack my things and get out of the house before they locked the door behind me."

I stopped to collect my thoughts and saw that Toni was also crying.

"What happened after that?"

"Laurel had an apartment. She and her roommate let me live with them until I could get my bearings. They could barely afford to feed themselves, but they took me in. I slept on their sofa for two months before I found a job and moved to Philadelphia. The first thing I did when I started getting a paycheck was to repay my parents the tuition money. There was no way I could live with myself, knowing that they had paid to help me begin my career. I didn't want them to have any connection to my life. Not that I was hurting them with my attitude. They felt the same way."

"Have you seen them since then?"

"No."

"Beth... God, that's awful." She pulled me into her arms. "I can't believe that they haven't been in touch with their own daughter in..." She stopped to do the math. "Over ten years. I'm sorry I brought this up. I suppose I don't always realize how lucky I am to have the family that I do."

Needing her comfort, I leaned in and kissed her.

"I want you to meet my family," she said. "They'll love you."

I made my best attempt at a smile and moved closer to her,

encircled in her arms as I rested my head on her chest. I finally had a place where I was loved.

Chapter Nine

June arrived in a thunderous fury. A front moved through Frederick, bringing storms that shook the windows of the studio. Fat, overzealous raindrops slapped against the glass, making the windows opaque. By early afternoon, the frightful weather had passed, but not before zapping the power at the office. I sent Bryce and Kristy home and worked off of the juice of my laptop battery as long as I could, hoping the power would come back on. It didn't.

When I arrived home, Toni's car was in the parking spot assigned to my apartment. A broad smile replaced the weather-induced scowl that had hung on my face all day. The sun hadn't yet set, and it cast a lovely orange glow over the neighborhood.

I had given her a key to my house, and I was happy to find that she had finally used it.

I parked behind Toni's Prius. *Now you're trapped, little lady.* The thought made me laugh as I yanked the strap of my briefcase over my shoulder and locked the car. I walked inside the building and climbed the stairs to my apartment. The front door was unlocked, and I hesitated for a moment. "I really, really hope this isn't a horror movie," I said out loud before twisting the knob and going inside.

The house was dim, the only light coming from the glow of candles scattered about. *No power at home, either.*

My mood threatened to turn south again, until I heard the faint clattering sounds coming from the kitchen. I found Toni sipping a glass of wine while setting the table. There were take-out containers behind her on the counter.

I stopped in the doorway. She looked up from what she was doing, and her smile brightened the room, and my heart.

"I thought that you probably didn't have power here, either, so when I got your text that you were planning on leaving the office early, I thought we could try to make the best of the situation." Her sweeping gesture included the candles, the food, and the table.

"Do you have power at your place?" I asked, surprised by the trouble she had gone to for me.

Her nose scrunched. "Nope."

"Stay here with me tonight?" My heart thumped once, then twice, while I waited for her response.

Her sexy, lopsided grin appeared. "I have an overnight bag in my trunk."

My chest tightened, and I felt a little lightheaded. I stood motionless, just watching her.

The sensual smile slipped from her face. "What's wrong, Beth? Was it—"

"I don't know how I lived before you came along."

I didn't even realize Toni had moved toward me until she pulled me into a close embrace.

"Oh, baby, I feel the same way about you," she cooed as she

pulled me in so close, I barely knew where I ended and she began.

I buried my face in her hair and breathed her in. She smelled like summer and wild honeysuckle. She smelled like home.

Toni pulled back and studied my face.

"Don't second guess. I want this, Toni. I want you." I kissed her, and drew her to me. I needed her.

Her lips met mine in an explosion of passion. All these months together had been building up to this, and I knew that the timing was right. I grasped Toni's hips and pulled her tight against me.

She groaned as she pressed her inner thigh against my leg. Her hands snaked around my waist and held fast.

A crackle of energy sizzled between us. Our ragged breathing was the only sound as we stood in the darkening kitchen.

"Upstairs?" I pleaded against her mouth.

She nodded, and held up a finger, indicating for me to wait while she picked up a candle to take with us and dimmed the rest with a soft blow to each.

I turned and took her hand in mine, hoping she wouldn't change her mind between the kitchen and my bedroom. Hands entwined, we climbed the steps to the loft.

A trickle of nervousness slid up my spine as we reached my bed and I turned to face Toni.

Her eyes were unique, almost gold in color, I thought, as I noted the yellow flecks dotting her brown eyes. Her lips, full and creamy soft, upturned in a slight smile. Her hair hid the shape of her face as it hung wildly around her head. I buried my fingers in the silkiness and combed them through the loose curls.

She watched me watching her, then slowly rubbed my back. The electricity of her touch prompted me to action, and I gently drew her to me and kissed her.

She met my kiss with such intensity that I gasped. As her tongue explored my mouth, she worked her hands under my blouse. Each sensation blended into the next as she moved to my neck, mouth open, and pressed her lips against my hot skin until I was sure I would die from the pleasure of it. Her hands shifted to my breasts.

My hands were involved in an exploration of their own, moving from Toni's hair to her face, down to her neck, shoulders, arms, and finally her breasts, which felt full in my hands.

She took a deep breath and murmured, "I know we both said we needed to go slow, but this feels right."

We stood together next to the bed, slowly undressing. The candle we had brought upstairs provided the light by which I now admired her body. The light of candle flames danced across Toni's fair skin as she revealed herself. A flush covered her neck and chest. A freckle just below her collarbone drew me to kiss her there. I nipped and kissed slowly down her chest until I reached the impediment of her bra. I reached behind and unclasped the garment and let it fall to the floor. Toni backed away and removed the rest of her clothing. She stood still, allowing me to take her in. I licked my lips as my eyes traveled from her face, to her breasts, and then downward. Her stomach was toned, and dotted by a trail of beauty marks. She was more lovely than I had imagined.

If I touched her, there would be no turning back. I had to ask, "Are you sure?"

Her nod was all the permission I needed. I pulled the comforter from the bed and lay back on the warm sheets, drawing her down with me.

Her hands went everywhere, caressing every part of my body before they moved on. Sometimes she would stop to ask "do you like this?" or "is this okay?"

My whimpers and an occasional soft "yes" were all the response she needed.

She moved above me, pressing her warmth against me. Her kisses tantalized my lips; her tongue met mine. I sighed as she moved slowly down my body, leaving scorching kisses along the way. Her mouth moved to my breasts, sucking, gently biting my nipple while her fingernails skimmed across the other. She tantalized my breasts until my sighs of pleasure told her that I couldn't bear it any longer, and then her hot, wet mouth moved slowly, too slowly, down to my legs, nibbling and kissing, leaving me weak.

My spine tingled from her incessant teasing. "Toni, please," I pleaded impatiently.

She looked up at me and grinned saucily before taking me into her mouth, tasting my passion.

After endless months of building tension, at the first touch of her tongue, my release bubbled up from within me. A soft cry left my lips as I lay back on the bed, my hips pumping against Toni's mouth. My fingers were tangled tightly in her hair, and I tugged her face closer to me. Within seconds, bright colors flashed behind my eyes, and I called out Toni's name as the orgasm shattered me. When my eyes were able to focus, Toni was beside me on the bed, smiling contentedly.

"You've done this before, haven't you?"

"Not with anyone as incredible as you. I plan on doing it many more times, just to be sure I get it right." She laughed. "I'm totally addicted to you, in case you haven't noticed."

I covered her body with mine. When I kissed her, I tasted and felt myself on her lips. I moved to her breasts, circling her nipples with my fingertips, stroking the tender flesh with my tongue.

I couldn't prolong the game of teasing her as she had done to me. I wanted to make her feel as good as she had made me feel.

I slid down toward the foot of the bed, then nudged her legs apart to kiss her inner thighs, moving toward her center. My mouth explored her before I tentatively entered her. Her rasping moan spurred me on.

Her hands stroked my hair, and her moan was constant as my fingers delved, caressed, and she cried out as her body stiffened in climax. She rocked and swayed for a moment before she lay still. After a few moments, she pulled me toward her, and I rested in her arms.

Chapter Ten

Laurel was standing on a chair, her backside directly in front of me. I snorted when I thought of how just a few short months earlier, seeing her in that position would have had me breaking out in a hormone-induced sweat, but now I just wanted my friend's butt away from my face. I envisioned using a thumbtack for a quick game of "pin the tail on your best friend."

"What's so funny? Hand me another tack." Laurel stole a quick glance at me before turning back to make sure the streamers she was hanging from her dining room ceiling were perfectly centered.

I ignored her question as I pried another tack from the packet and handed it to her. I was the wingman who handed her the thumbtacks.

Will walked by and playfully slapped her butt as he grinned at me.

I rolled my eyes and provided the teasing I knew was expected of me. "God, would you guys please get a room? You've been together for like, what...fifty years. Shouldn't you be sick of each other by now?"

"Give me a break," Laurel replied from her elevated perch. "I've had to witness that kind of behavior between you and your girlfriend several times. It's probably a good thing Toni is away at that conference, or you'd be sitting here making goo-goo eyes at her instead of helping us set up." She turned and made a face worthy of her daughters. "Besides, who says you're the only ones who can get a little action?"

Girlfriend. It was the first time I'd heard it out loud in reference to me and Toni. I loved it.

Will laughed and then took a sip from his bottle of beer. He had just finished mowing the lawn in preparation for Kira's eleventh birthday party, which was scheduled to begin in a couple of hours.

"Countdown to chaos," Will glanced at his watch, "one hour and forty-eight minutes. Are you guys okay with the decorating? I need to hop in the shower."

Laurel climbed down from the chair and gave her husband a quick kiss. "Yes, we're finished. Go get cleaned up."

Will left the room just as Kira came bounding in from the back yard, closely followed by Becca.

Kira ran to me and hugged me around the waist, and I realized it wouldn't be long before she was grown enough to want to borrow my clothes. I loved her at the age she was at — not so young that constant care was needed, and not yet old enough to have hormonal moods.

I hugged her to me. "What's up, kiddo? Ready for your party?"

She stepped back with a smile. "Yes, but I'm more excited about my gift. When do I get it?"

I smiled and mussed her hair. "You have to wait until after you open everyone else's gifts. I told you that earlier, but I commend you for trying to trick me."

She sighed dramatically and flounced toward the stairs, while commenting over her shoulder, "Well, you're old, so I thought maybe you would forget that you told me that and give me my present now."

I looked up at Laurel, sure my wide eyes conveyed my surprise.

"Well, she's learning from the best. You have to admit that." Laurel shook her head. "She gets her sense of humor from you, so you have no one to blame but yourself. Let's go get a beer."

I followed her to the back yard, where lawn chairs and picnic tables were set up for the party. She took two bottles of beer from the cooler and handed one to me. I took the beer, grabbed my favorite deck chair, and settled back into the soft canvas. l ran the icy cold glass against my cheek. It was going to be a hot afternoon. I closed my eyes and relished the first sip of the cold beer sliding down my throat.

"I love how you interact with the girls. I always hoped that as they grew older, they would know they could turn to you as much as to me or Will, and I'm happy to say, I think that's happened. They love you to death. Sometimes I think they like you more than they like me." Laurel frowned.

"You're going to get wrinkles if you keep doing that." I tapped her bicep with my cold bottle of beer, and she jumped. "That's only because I don't have to discipline them. I buy them things like iPods for their birthdays, of course they like me," I laughed.

"Oh, Beth, seriously? An iPod? You spoil them."

"I like spoiling them. They're like the kids I'll never have, so why not do what I can for them?"

Laurel's brow crinkled. "What are your plans as far as Toni's concerned? You've only been together a couple of months, but you seem very content."

"I am."

"I thought you'd be living together by now." She poked my leg with her toe. "I've never seen you this happy in all the years I've known you. I guess I know how to pick 'em, huh?"

"You do." I nodded. "She's the one, that's for sure." Even had I'd tried, I wouldn't have been able to stop smiling every time I thought of Toni.

"Good, I'm glad. You've been through a lot, and you deserve to be over the moon. So, when do you think you'll move in together? What about marriage? You guys can legally marry here now. Have you given that any thought?"

"We've been talking about getting a place together. In fact, I think we're going to start looking for a house to buy before school resumes in the fall. Both of our apartments are just a little too small for the two of us. Not sure about marriage." I let the last statement hang without further comment.

Laurel nodded. "What about kids? You're both great with Kira and Becca. I think having a baby or two would be a logical thing for you both."

I considered her question for a moment. "Not sure. I haven't really considered it seriously. I like having Toni to myself. I like being able to go out whenever we want or to be alone at home. I'm not sure I'd want to share her. Besides, with the mess my parents are, I don't know if I want to take on the responsibility. There are too many ways to screw up and ruin a kid's life." I flashed back to my first date with Toni, when she mentioned wanting to have a family one day. The subject hadn't come up since.

"Don't *ever* compare yourself to your parents in any way. You would never mess up the way they did. And by mess up, I mean by not accepting you the way you are. As far as raising a wonderful human being, they actually got that part right." Anger clouded her face. She tipped her bottle of beer and took a healthy chug.

I loved this protective side of my friend. "I like you when you say nice things to me," I joked. "Keep it up, and I'll let you continue to be my friend."

She laughed and rose from her chair. "Sit here and have another beer. I need to straighten up a bit before everyone gets here. The sooner we get this party over with, the sooner we can polish off this cooler of beer."

Chapter Eleven

It had been an arduous day at the studio. I had spent most of it on the wrong side of a telephone shouting match with a client. Bryce sent a brochure to the printer and ordered the wrong number of them, and the customer had made it clear he was not happy. His displeasure was understandable, but what I faulted him for was the way he communicated it. I hated yelling, and there was certainly no place for it in business.

Now the tendons in my neck felt as tightly strung as the cables used to suspend the Golden Gate Bridge. I could barely turn my head as I zipped my car in and out of traffic, finding the fastest route to Toni's apartment. My girlfriend had promised me a romantic dinner and a massage, and I did not want to be late for either. The thought generated my first genuine smile of the day.

I flipped the satellite radio on and jabbed at the controls. I needed something to release some of the stress. I found Concrete Blonde's *Still in Hollywood* about halfway through the song, and cranked the volume. "Yeahhhhh!" I pounded the steering wheel with my palm as I sang along. At least it was my version of singing.

Even the fact that the closest parking spot I could find was a block and a half away from Toni's apartment building couldn't dampen my good mood. The day was hot, but arid, making the heat more bearable. I was thankful for the lack of the usual humidity in the air. I thought about how this glorious day could have been ruined by an idiot with a temper, and I hoped Bryce hadn't let the incident affect the rest of his day.

I jogged up the stairs to Toni's apartment and used my key to let myself in. A pleasant aroma of what I hoped was dinner beckoned me into the kitchen. I tried to decipher what I was smelling. Spices, maybe chiles. Definitely something tomatoey. Cinnamon? My stomach gurgled.

Toni was peering into a pot on the stove, but when she heard me come in, she put the spoon down and turned toward me with a broad smile.

"This is a raid. Just cooperate with everything I tell you, and no one will get hurt. At least not in a bad way." I wiggled my eyebrows, trying for sexy but achieving only comical.

Toni giggled. "You're so funny." She opened her arms and moved toward me.

Grinning, I moved into her embrace. "What do we have here? It smells so good." As if to underscore my appreciation, my stomach rumbled.

"Molé Poblano with rice and tortillas."

Gurgle. "I honestly don't know how you were still available when I came along. Lesbians are stupid."

Toni barely managed a smile.

My curiosity was piqued and my comedic ego bruised. "What's wrong? I thought that was pretty funny."

"I'm doing my best to create a romantic evening for two." Toni released me to reach for a glass of wine identical to hers, which she handed to me.

"I'd say your best is pretty damn good.

Toni seated herself at the table. "I want to run something by you, but I was hoping to feed and seduce you beforehand."

My brow furrowed in puzzlement.

She sat and toyed with her wine glass, running a finger around and around along the rim. I expected to hear a tune if she kept it up. She ran her tongue across her bottom lip, which accentuated the dimple in her right cheek.

I didn't care what she had to tell me. All I could think of was running my tongue over that dimple and then moving to other areas of her body. I was a goner for sure.

"I'm going home to visit my family before school starts again." She watched me with one eye squinted shut. This was a sign that she had dropped the first shoe, and the other was coming soon.

"Okaaayyy, what does that mean?" Thinking I grasped her meaning, I gasped, "Are you trying to tell me that you're not coming back? Is that it? Because if it's something I've done, I can—"

Toni was off her chair in a flash, and clutching my arms.

"No, no, no, no, no! Oh my God, Beth, you have to stop thinking that every time I open my mouth, I'm breaking up with you!" She rubbed my arms and tipped her head to make sure we had eye contact. "Beth, honey, I love you. I'm not going anywhere."

I took a deep breath and tried to shrug off my embarrassment. She was right. At every turn, I expected her to end our relationship.

"What is it then? Why do you look like you want to tell me something bad?"

"I want you to go with me." Her lips turned up in a slight smile. She blinked once, then twice, her long lashes kissing her skin.

She did that on purpose. No fair.

I may be slow at times, but I finally understood where the conversation was going. Unable to formulate words, my mouth just hung open. I had known that meeting Toni's family was inevitable, but the very thought of it caused a knot in the pit of my stomach. Parents and I did not go well together. I moved away from her and sipped my wine.

"My parents already like you from what I've told them and from talking to you on the phone."

I swallowed the last of my wine and moved into her arms again. "You're right, I know. It's just that I'm not accustomed to having a girlfriend who has normal, stable parents. All the parents I've been introduced to would have preferred meeting a boyfriend. And then we have my parents. Enough said."

It was true. In the several years I had been with Julie, I hadn't once met her parents. I never knew why, but I had no great desire to meet them, so I never asked.

"I know, baby, but this time will be different. Mom and Dad don't care if I love a boy or a girl, as long as I have someone who's good to me. They just want me to be happy." She kissed my forehead. "And you make me happy."

I managed a weak smile. "I'll just be a bit edgy until it's over with."

"That's understandable. Now let's eat so we can move on to other things." She grinned wickedly. "Maybe I can help take that edge off."

"You're devious. You knew I wouldn't say no if you fed me molé. Evil woman."

She smiled proudly as she turned back to the stove.

"There had better be flan for dessert."

~ ~ ~

The wind whooshed past us, tangling our hair. The ocean air was freeing and filled my car with end of summertime smells. Toni and I were on our first road trip together, going to Delaware to visit her parents. It was just the two of us, and tens of thousands of others headed to the beach for a last desperate summer getaway. The crawl through the corridor between home and the beaches had been trying, but after getting beyond the major highways, I was able to slip the car into high gear and roll smoothly toward our destination.

Piloting the Jag over long distances would usually have made me happy and carefree, instead my stomach was in knots and the tension was threatening to cause a headache. Despite my artistic nature, I had plenty of common sense, and it was telling me that I was being silly. I meet new people every day in my profession, and they never make me nervous. *Well, rarely.*

This shouldn't have been any different. *Yeah, right.*

Toni's family lived in downtown Rehoboth Beach, a notoriously gay-friendly town on the Delaware shore. I chuckled when Toni told me that. No wonder her parents were so accepting of her sexuality; they lived in the gay mecca of the Mid-Atlantic region. Couldn't get more gay-friendly than that. They owned and operated a bed and breakfast, which they had purchased after Toni and her brother had left home.

As we neared town, Toni moved her hand from my thigh to my shoulder and gently kneaded. I smiled wanly in her direction, trying to show her, and myself, that I was not afraid.

"We're really close now!"

My stomach did a flip then a flop.

The ocean in the air around us was cool, and sticky with a salty tang. I could feel the salt settling on my skin as the moist air enveloped me. I imagined myself on the beach — the roughness of the beach towel on my back, the sound of seagulls flying overhead and swooping down to steal a French fry or a bit of ice cream cone. I could hear children shrieking with joy, and waves roaring toward the beach. My heart slowed, and I took a deep breath. If her parents hated me, I could spend the long weekend lying on the beach, baking from the outside in and fending off the birds.

"Beth, it's going to be okay. They will love you."

I glanced over at Toni and saw the compassion in her gaze. She could always tell what I was feeling. I loved that about her. I nodded as I turned my attention back to the road.

Toni leaned over and kissed my temple. "Turn left at this

next light, and it's at the end of the road, on the right."

Flip, flop.

I slowed the car on the residential street and cruised toward the end of the road as instructed. Large Victorian homes lined both sides of the road, and I wondered if they were all B&Bs, and if so, how Toni's parents managed to make any money.

Toni directed me into a spot about three quarters of the way down the street.

Her excitement had been palpable during the entire drive, but she still surprised me when she jumped from the car as soon as the Jag came to a complete stop.

She scurried to the back of the car. "Pop the trunk," she called.

In the time it took me to put the car into neutral, set the brake, and turn the ignition off, she pulled one suitcase and then another from the trunk and set them on the sidewalk. I was amazed.

Toni's smile was luminous as she stood on the sidewalk next to the car, waiting for me to join her. I locked the car and pulled my suitcase along beside me with one hand while Toni clutched my other hand.

"It'll be fine, I promise." She gave me a quick peck on the lips.

Not once did she tell me I was being childish or reprimand me for feeling nervous. Instead, she did everything she could to calm my nerves and ease my insecurities. I made a mental note to thank her later.

I wiped my sweaty palms on my shorts and followed her to

the house on the corner, comparing it to the others as we approached. How did people not accidentally go to the wrong house every night after work? As far as I could tell, every house matched each of the others. The large, inviting porch held several cushy chairs, perfect for falling into after a day at the beach. Banisters painted in a hideous green fought visually with tall columns of pink and blue. It looked like a kid had vomited cotton candy.

The door opened, and a middle-aged couple hurried out to greet us. I noticed instantly that Toni had her mother's smile. She beamed at me the way her daughter did, and the one dimple was also present on this pleasant older version of Toni's face. I thanked God that I didn't also find her mother's lopsided grin sexy. We climbed the stairs, and I held out my hand, only to be tugged into a welcoming embrace, first from Toni's mother, Grace, then by Rich, her dad.

Toni and I followed her parents into the house. I found that the garish exterior of the home was not a true representation of Grace's and Rich's style. The walls were rich earth tones, and bamboo flooring complemented the deep hued area rugs in each room. The foyer led to a living room on the left and a library of sorts on the right. I was drawn to this room. I gazed in at the massive marble fireplace, which was flanked on each side by bookshelves stacked to capacity, and decided instantly that Toni and I would need to come to visit again in the winter so I could take advantage of this room. I saw myself settled in a fat brocade chair, my sock-covered feet tucked under me as I sipped hot chocolate and listened to the firewood popping in the warm fireplace.

Toni roused me from my imaginings with a gentle palm against my back. "Let's take our bags upstairs, okay?"

With a smile for her parents, I lifted my bag and went up the stairs after Toni. Even the staircase offered glimpses into the owners' personalities.

I slowed to take in the family photos hanging on the wall. Near the main floor, I saw a pint-sized Toni in several photos, laughing with a boy I assumed was her brother. In more than a few of the shots, her hair was disheveled and her knees scabbed. As I climbed, Toni aged in the photos, photos probably from her years in high school, with friends and family, growing more and more beautiful with each year that went by. Photos of her parents were sprinkled in alongside these childhood snapshots, a happy young couple posing with their arms lovingly around each other's waists. I didn't realize I'd stopped until Toni cleared her throat to get my attention.

"Are you coming with me, or will you be sleeping on the stairs this weekend?" The lines that I found so attractive formed around her eyes as she smiled.

I could tell she was happy to be home, even though this wasn't the house she'd grown up in. I hurried after her, excited to see more of the house, particularly the room we would be sharing for the weekend.

I was beginning to relax, and it crossed my mind that I might actually enjoy myself this visit. Toni's parents seemed pleased to meet me, and my first impression was that they were not in the least judgmental.

Our room was modern yet cozy. I was delighted with the Vincents' sense of style, happy to see that they hadn't felt compelled to retain the Victorian look of the house, as most owners probably would.

We rolled our cases to the closet to be unpacked later on. I flopped onto the bed, weary from the long ride and the stress I had let build up inside of me.

Grinning, Toni came over to the bed and lay beside me. She ran her fingernails across my abdomen. "What do you think so far?"

She sounded breathless. Was she worried about my reaction to her parents?

I cupped her cheek. "So far, so good. I didn't know what to expect as far as beds would go."

She turned her head toward me, fighting a grin. "You seriously thought we'd get here and there would be no beds?"

"You know what I mean — sleeping arrangements." I poked her in the ribs, and she squealed. "That'll teach you to try to be funny. *I'm* the funny one in this family."

Toni's eyes sparkled. "You don't have to worry about sleeping arrangements here. My parents have always treated my brother and me as adults. Their viewpoint is that it's up to us what the sleeping arrangements should be. They have never been weird about that." Her fingertips trailed over my cheek. "Don't worry, okay? We're here to have fun. You're not being judged or tested."

The woman was a mind reader.

"I want to spend some time with the folks, but why don't we go for a romantic walk on the beach after dinner tonight?"

"Sounds fantastic." I gave her lips a quick peck, and then she rose from the bed and began to unpack our bags. *So much for rest.*

~ ~ ~

By the time we settled into bed, it was well past the witching hour and I was bone-weary. The firm mattress felt good beneath my tired body.

Toni stretched out alongside me, her hair fanning out over her pillow. Her eyes questioned me, searching for an answer to an unspoken question. Her lip was curled in that crooked smile of hers, and her eyes danced playfully. This woman couldn't *not* be sexy if she tried. My heart thumped in my chest, as my libido tried to convince my tired brain to stay awake just a little bit longer.

"My parents love you. Should I say 'I told you so,' or just stick out my tongue?"

"Hmmm. well, I love you the most when your tongue is sticking out."

Toni poked me in the ribs, hitting one of my few ticklish spots.

I jumped and wriggled away from her. "Stop it! Your parents will think we're doing something X-rated."

Her laugh was infectious. "So what if they do? They know we're a couple. They know we're in here all alone in bed together." Her perfect eyebrows waggled.

"I'm not so sure your mom knows what goes on between us.

You think she's so accepting of you being a lesbian, but I think that's only because she thinks we sit around and exchange recipes and give each other pecks on the cheeks."

I was only partly kidding. Her mother thought our relationship was so cute, I didn't see how she could understand the reality of it.

"Stop! You're being ridiculous." Toni laughed. "Oh my God, she does not think that. Now go to sleep." She gave me a quick kiss and rolled over with her back to me, making it clear that the subject was closed.

"Okay, but I still think I'm right. I pretty sure that I heard she has us signed up for a game of dress-up tomorrow afternoon, with a teddy bear tea party afterwards."

I felt the bed move as Toni laughed quietly. Turning off the bedside light cast the room into darkness except for the glow of the moon through the skylight. I rolled onto my side, wrapped my arm around Toni, and kissed the nape of her neck. "I love you, and your family."

Toni placed her hand over mine and squeezed. "That means a lot to me. I love you, too." In less than a minute, I could hear the soft, steady breathing that told me she was asleep.

~ ~ ~

Toni's parents had closed their B&B for the weekend so that there would be no distractions from their family reunion, which continued into Saturday with the arrival of Toni's brother Scott, and his wife and two children. They were as laid back as Toni was, which relaxed me immediately. The meet-the-family jitters were finally subsiding.

"Are you up for an evening out?" Toni asked. "Dad's treating for dinner."

"Sure."

The beach-themed seafood restaurant felt cozy, and I absorbed the surroundings and the company. It felt natural to take part in the easy conversation going on around me. It was clear that Toni's family loved her unconditionally and accepted her completely. Her carefree interaction with Scott was evidence that they were especially close. Toni was telling the story of our first meeting, and I had to smile at her version of our blind date.

"She walked into the restaurant at least a half hour late, probably more than that." Her dark eyes sparkled in my direction. "Laurel was a nervous wreck, positive that Beth was a no-show, and I was getting a bit upset at being stood up." She chuckled at my look of surprise.

"You never told me that!"

"But she walked in…I knew it was her right away…and I instantly forgave her when I saw how beautiful she was. And she was so flustered and apologetic about being late, that I couldn't help but fall in love."

I fought a blush as Grace and Rich laughed at Toni's story, which I was sure they'd heard already.

With a sly glimmer in his eyes that he directed at his older sister, Scott said, "That's a far cry from the blind date you were set up on in high school. Do you remember that?" he teased.

"Has she told you about her date with Andy Simmons in

eleventh grade, Beth?"

I played along. "No. I'm sure I would have remembered hearing about that."

"Thank you so much for reminding me." Toni buried her face in her hands. "Let's just say that Andy was the last boy I dated before fully coming to terms with being gay," she explained.

"You always used to say that going out with him was what did it," Rich added with a laugh.

"He sounds like something." I said.

Toni winked. "Baby, he had nothing on you."

~ ~ ~

When we returned from dinner, we sat in the living room for a while, enjoying cocktails and continuing our conversation. I'd had a few more drinks than I was used to, and my head was swimming. Now the hour was late, and everyone had retired to their rooms. Toni was sitting in bed, watching me undress.

"Your dad makes a killer mojito." I realized my words had slurred a bit. As I sat on the bed to take off my jeans, I asked, "How did I do?"

"I'd say you've made a definite impression." She pushed a lock of hair behind her ear and leaned back against the headboard, which was cushioned with pillows. "They like you. I can tell."

I slipped underneath the covers and lay alongside her. "How can you tell?"

"Because I asked them."

"You didn't!"

"Yes, I did." Toni answered. "At least I asked Mom. She said 'she's very nice and it's obvious how happy she makes you. That's good enough for me.'"

"I'm glad. I like them too. They're not nearly as scary as I thought they would be." That earned me a laugh.

I fluffed my pillows and settled in, covering myself with the comforter. Toni turned off the bedside lamp and then snuggled next to me, kissing my neck.

"What are you doing?" I asked suspiciously.

"If you can't tell, I'm not doing it right." Toni wrapped her arms around me. "I want you."

"Honey, I don't know how to tell you this, but your parents are in the next room...or down the hallway, or downstairs. Thanks to the alcohol I'd consumed, *downstairs* sounded more like *downshhhtairs*, but I continued. "Honestly, this house is huge, so I'm not sure where they are, but I'm pretty certain they're under this roof. Your brother and his family are here somewhere, too, which normally wouldn't be a problem, but you're very vocal, to be blunt."

"I'll be quiet," she purred.

"That's impossible. Besides, I feel uncomfortable knowing that your mother and father are here. With them knowing what I did to their daughter, how can I look them in the eye tomorrow?"

"Oh please! They're not naive. They know we make love."

"I know that they know. It's just...you know!"

"No, I don't know." Toni laughed. "But you're adorable." She kissed me then, melting my insides. I knew that she would have her way, and that regardless of whether her parents were in the room next to us or directly under the bed, we would make love.

~ ~ ~

Despite the lateness of the hour at which we had finally gone to sleep, Toni and I rose at dawn to take a walk on the beach together before the others woke. The morning was crisp, and I could smell the ocean in the air the second we stepped onto the front porch. Toni took my hand and I followed her lead, unsure of which direction we should head. The beach was a mere three block stroll from the bed and breakfast.

As we drew nearer, I could hear the waves gently lapping at the shore. The seagulls soared overhead, dipping now and then to grab a tidbit from under the waves. I laughed as I remembered an outing on the Santa Monica Pier when a seagull swooped down and snatched a churro that had been halfway to my mouth. Not wanting to spoil the perfect silence, I made a mental note to share the story with Toni later.

Toni saw my contented smile. Catching my eye, she said, "Thank you for last night."

"You have bed head, darlin'," I ribbed, tousling her hair.

"That's from you slamming my head repeatedly into the headboard," she said dryly.

"I didn't hear any complaints last night. Actually, I didn't hear too much of anything. I didn't realize you could be so quiet." I laughed, and she pulled me against her side and kissed me.

"I think I could live here," I said, mostly to myself, as we continued our walk.

Toni's eyebrow rose along with one corner of her mouth. "You could?"

That crooked grin always made my heart stammer. "Mmm hmmm, I think I could."

We reached the shore, and we walked along its very edge, our sandaled feet cooled by the waves that came ashore every few seconds. The purple sky turned blue and the sun blazed on the horizon, and we held hands as we strolled in silence. No words were necessary. I knew I had found my home with Toni, and she knew it as well.

Chapter Twelve

I have always hated winter, and the first one spent with Toni was brutal. By early October, my internal thermostat told me that my beloved summer was long over. The icy air constantly assaulted my skin, and my mood had a tendency to match my physical discomfort.

My spirits improved before the holidays when we moved into the house of our dreams. We enlisted the help of Laurel and Will, Bryce, Kristy and her husband Allen, and a few of Toni's friends from school to help us unpack and arrange our belongings. Laurel's girls were with a sitter, so they wouldn't be in the way.

In a few back-breaking hours, all of our earthly possessions had been situated in our new residence, and we had officially settled into our first home together, except for the boxes that still needed to be unpacked. We were a tired but happy bunch as we celebrated with pizza and bottles of champagne. By the time our meal was finished, I was thoroughly exhausted. I found it impossible to move from my spot on the gleaming hardwood floor in the living room. Luckily, our fellow movers took the hint and began to depart. Laurel and Will were the last to leave. Toni and I walked them to the door and hugged them warmly.

"I'm so grateful to you both," I said. "Not just for today, but for everything."

"Don't be silly," Will said. "You know we would do anything for you, and you'd do the same for us."

I had always been convinced that Laurel had found the one and only flawless man on the face of the Earth, and he had just proven it to me.

"You're pretty terrific for a guy," I said. "I love you both."

We hugged again, and they were off, bundled in their down coats. I stood on our front steps and watched them until they drove away. The sky looked very blue. Snow would come soon.

I went back into the house and looked for Toni. I found her in the kitchen, tossing paper plates into the trash and setting used glasses in the sink. She looked as exhausted as I felt. I stood behind her and wrapped my arms around her waist, then kissed the back of her neck. She turned in my arms and wrapped her arms around me.

"Let's go take a nice warm shower together in our new place," I suggested.

"Mmmmmm, you don't have to ask me twice. Some hot water would feel so good on my shoulders right now."

I followed Toni to the bathroom, sole audience to her striptease as she began peeling off her clothes along the way. *Lord have mercy.* I quickly removed my clothes and ran the water as she finished undressing and stepped behind the glass shower door with me. I was sure I could never grow tired of seeing her naked body.

The steaming water hit my skin in fat droplets. It was what I had been craving all day. I took Toni into my arms as the water soaked us. Using the bar of soap, I washed her back and arms, and then myself, washing off every last bit of the sweaty film that covered me.

I angled the shower head to rinse us both, and felt the heat of Toni's tongue press through the water against my neck. The feel of her mouth set up a flutter in my belly. Despite my extreme fatigue, my body responded to her touch.

Toni settled one hand on my breast and the other between my legs. She moaned when she found my velvet wetness. Her fingers slid inside me, working steadily. My legs became weak, and it wasn't only from the fatigue of moving dozens of boxes all day long.

As my orgasm erupted, I propped myself against the shower wall, pulling Toni along with me. She raised a hand to steady me, kissing me hungrily as my body shook from the delicious waves engulfing me. She held me securely until I could stand on my own.

Tears rose in my eyes as happiness settled in around me. I had a new house, and a partner who loved me. "I love you, baby. I always will," I sighed when I finally caught my breath.

Toni kissed me, her tongue tangling with mine, our mouths merging underneath the spray of water.

I guided her to where I had been standing and lowered myself to my knees. The water drummed on my back as I kissed her thighs, working my way up to her center. My lips met heat and moisture, and Toni moaned. I moved deeper inside her, touching, tasting.

She braced her hands on my shoulders for support as I kissed her most private area, lavishing my love on her with my mouth, pressing my fingers into her, listening to her gasping. Her nails pressed painfully into my skin as her breath quickened and she cried out.

I stood and held her close. When we both had recovered, I shut the water off and scrambled out into the living room in search of towels, which we had forgotten to bring into the bathroom with us.

I wrapped a towel around Toni and then one around myself, and led her to our new bedroom. She settled into bed while I moved through each room in the house, turning lights off and making sure each door was locked before I climbed into bed next to her and fell into the deep sleep of exhaustion.

THREE YEARS LATER
Chapter Thirteen

"I want to have a family with you."

Toni and I were propped up in bed together on a rain-drenched Sunday morning. The newspaper lay scattered between us about the bed in sections, damp because it had been deposited on the partially uncovered front porch.

My first thought was that Toni had begun to tell me about something she was reading in the news. I waited for the rest of the story.

Her reading glasses perched high on her nose, and she held the Lifestyles section of the newspaper in her lap. Her eyes were wide, and her bottom lip puffed out in encouragement for me to respond the way she wanted.

I had seen the look before.

Realization struck. "What are you talking about? We have a family. We are a family." Where the hell was this coming from? *Blast* The Washington Post. *They must have run another article on lesbians having babies.*

Toni tossed the paper to the foot of the bed and turned so she could straddle my hips. Her eyes danced playfully as her palms pinned my shoulders to the headboard.

"Children!" She grinned. "I want to have a baby with you."

I was pinned and stunned. The thought of raising a child gave rise to various responses, the central one being panic. I stalled for time to sort out this new information. "You've never mentioned wanting children."

"That's not true," she countered. "I told you on our first date that I wanted to have a baby someday."

I remembered her saying it, but either I hadn't taken her seriously or I didn't expect the subject to come up again. But seriously...on our first date? There should have been a warning that the conversation would resume years later. I envisioned Toni sliding a disclosure toward me on our first date, asking me to sign and date it. I smothered a giggle.

"Sorry, I guess I lost the notes I was taking that night." To lighten the mood, I looked around and pretended to search for a misplaced notebook.

Toni either didn't notice or deliberately ignored the evasion in my response. "Come on, I've brought it up several times since then."

"All I know about children is what I've seen with Becca and Kira, and that's enough to make me want to turn and run," I teased.

"What are you saying? They're sweet kids." She bent to nibble my ear, which was a sure sign she expected to get her way.

Children. It was something I had never really thought about. Now, thanks to this woman planted on my lap, the lesbian baby boom was about to explode right into my life. Maybe things could be worse, but they definitely could not get any stranger. I was perplexed.

Seriously? Three years into our relationship and Toni decides to throw this at me out of nowhere?

"You're right, you have mentioned that you love kids and would love to have your own, but you've never come right out and said, 'let's have a baby.' Why is this coming up now?"

Her clear brown eyes bored into mine. I had seen her do this many times over the years. It was like she could look right through my eyes into my brain and read exactly what I was thinking.

"Why now?" she repeated in a musing tone, as if she hadn't actually thought it out. "Number one, because we've had time to build a solid relationship. Number two, we have money and security. And the main reason is because I'm not getting any younger. I'll probably have more difficulty conceiving now than I would have at thirty. Why not now?" she asked, getting directly to the point.

We had never discussed the specifics of having children, and I had no idea how she planned on going about it. I hoped that it wouldn't involve us sitting down to have a little talk with Will, or even Bryce, for that matter.

"I'm not saying no. I'm not even saying not now. You just threw me for a loop. How do you intend to conceive?"

"Well, that's my point. We need to discuss what route we should take. There's a fertility clinic connected with one of the hospitals in Montgomery County that I've heard good things about. I was thinking that we'd start there."

She had it all figured out, it seemed.

She rose from the bed and grabbed her robe from the back of the door. "I need to take a shower. I'll let you think about what we've talked about." She smiled radiantly and slipped from the room, leaving me with sudden vertigo.

It would have to be the world's longest shower for me to absorb everything she had left me with. Instead, I rolled over and willed myself back to sleep. What seemed like only a minute later, Toni emerged from the shower and shook me gently from my sleep.

"How about getting dressed, and we can run down to Golden's to talk about this?" she suggested with an engaging smile.

I knew she was trying to appease me by suggesting my favorite coffee shop. I grimaced, but I nodded my head as I threw off the covers.

"Give me fifteen minutes," I said, trudging to the bathroom.

~ ~ ~

Half an hour later, Toni and I sat across from one another at a small corner table in Golden's. I held my cup like a lifeline, grasping it with both hands. Toni spoke, while I just stared into the milky brew.

"Beth, sweetie, I've always told you I want children. Despite your reaction, this should not be a surprise to you." I still did not meet her gaze. "I've seen you with Laurel's kids, and with my brother's, as well. You're a pro."

I looked up briefly. "All that proves is that I make a super aunt."

Toni sighed and sipped her coffee before trying another tack. "I'm not saying this is something I want to do tomorrow, Beth. But it is something I want. It may not happen for six months or a year. It may never happen at all, but I want to try. I want *us* to try, baby. I want you to be the one I experience this with. We promised each other forever, I don't want this with anyone but you."

My stony heart melted. The look on her face reinforced how important this was to her, and I knew then how much she loved me, but none of that changed the way I felt.

I attempted a weak smile. "Give me some time to adjust to this, Toni. You've given me a lot to absorb for one day."

"I know I have." She rubbed my arm. "I'll give you some time."

I pushed my coffee cup to the center of the table. The acid in my stomach had ruined any chance of me finishing it.

~ ~ ~

Laurel and I were seated at a small table on the patio of a local cafe we frequented. It was the weekend following Toni's astonishing announcement that she wanted us to become co-mothers, and my head was still in a muddle.

"What kind of parent do you think I'd be?" I asked distractedly as I sipped an iced latté while Laurel scanned her menu.

"I'm not sure." She peered over her menu. "But then again, I failed Hypothetical Questions 101." She grinned, until she noticed my disturbed state. She folded her arms, suddenly serious. "Why are you asking?"

"Toni has decided that we want a baby." I smiled lamely.

Laurel appeared confused, and understandably so, I thought. "How could she decide that you both want a baby?"

"That's not what I meant. She wants one, and I don't know what I want," I clarified.

Laurel closed her menu and set it on the table. She rested her chin on her hand and examined me a little too closely for my taste, making me regret that I'd brought the subject up.

"You're not happy with this latest development, I take it?"

"I don't know what I feel," I countered honestly. "My blood turned to ice the instant the words were out of her mouth. That is, as soon as I realized she was serious. I'm not ready for this!" I whined.

Laurel laughed and set her cup onto its saucer with a clatter. "What's this about? How many responsibilities do you have now?" She held up her fingers to count on. "You own and manage your own company. You've been part of a happy relationship for how long now...almost four years? God, you're beginning to make me look bad, and I'm considered the stable, mature one!"

I laughed despite myself.

"You love Becca and Kira like they're your own kids. You can do this! If..." She watched me over the rim of her cup as she sipped her drink. "If it's what you want. Don't do this for Toni alone."

"I wouldn't—"

"Yes, you would. I know you, and I know you'd do anything for that woman. But this isn't the time to be selfless. Raising a child is an enormous thing, and you should only do it if it's right for both of you." Taking stock of my abject expression, she added, "Toni will understand. It's what she'd want."

I spent many long hours mulling over the situation. I had never consciously considered becoming a parent, and if Toni hadn't expressed a desire to have children, I would have happily gone about my life without ever even considering parenthood.

In the time that we had been together, Toni and I hadn't faced any serious threats to our relationship. We argued like anyone else, but always managed to resolve any issues that cropped up. Our worst moments occurred because I learned early in life to not discuss any worries that I had, and that carried over into my relationships. On the opposite end of the spectrum, I would tease Toni that her upbringing taught her to confer with me whenever something even as trivial as a hangnail occurred. Somehow Toni had learned to deal with my silence when I was confronted with an obstacle in my life, something other women I had been involved with could never get past.

In the two weeks it took me to reach a decision, I kept my thoughts to myself as I worried about the consequences of having the responsibility of parenting a child. I took in my surroundings in an entirely different context than before. I watched intently as Toni interacted with Kira and Becca. Although they were now nearing their pubescent years, I had to admit that Toni was a natural with them. She was as instinctively maternal as she had been when they were younger.

~ ~ ~

One weekend afternoon, Toni sat at Laurel's kitchen table, braiding Kira's hair before turning her loose to walk to her best friend's house. She glanced up briefly and saw me watching her, and she smiled radiantly.

I knew what she was thinking, and returned her smile. I loved this woman more than I had ever loved another living soul. She was my lover, my best friend, and my rock. In the years that we'd been together, she had lifted me up when I was down, and had counted on me to do the same for her. She was my family when I had none. I planned on being with her for the rest of my life, and I would do anything for her. If she wanted a baby, I wouldn't hold her back.

"We can do this," she said.

And at last my heart agreed with her.

Chapter Fourteen

I was relieved that my decision was made, and knowing how happy it would make Toni, I planned a special evening to share it with her.

"You wouldn't mind getting the estimate ready for this job, would you, Bryce? I need to run home and get dinner started before Toni gets there, and I'm already running late."

Seated in a plush chair in front of my desk, Bryce rubbed his trim beard and appeared deep in thought. "Hmmm...it's not an anniversary, although I do believe it's the right time of the year for that." Grinning wickedly, he continued. "You must have done something wrong, if you're making amends by preparing a sumptuous feast."

I pursed my lips, as if in thought, then said, "You should have warned me when you interviewed for your position that I'd have to explain my every action from the day I hired you until the end of time. If you must know, Toni and I have been discussing having a baby, and I've decided it's something I'm willing to do. I want to tell Toni over a romantic dinner."

Bryce's eyes were almost as large as his mouth, which hung open in surprise.

"And before you get any bright ideas, that would be a

romantic dinner for two. You're not invited," I warned.

"A baby!" Bryce yelped.

"Shhh! I don't want everyone to know yet."

"But that's wonderful! Please let me be the godfather," he pleaded.

"Bryce, we're only in the first stage of development here. We have a lot of work ahead of us, and it's not a sure thing. What if Toni's one of those women who can't conceive?"

"Then it'll be up to you to carry the baby," he said matter-of-factly.

I glanced at him to gauge his seriousness. He wasn't laughing. "Not an option," I rose from my seat and gathered my belongings. "Seriously, Bryce, please don't tell anyone."

He rose and enveloped me in one of his crushing hugs. "I'll keep quiet, I promise. Thank you for sharing your good news with me." He smiled happily.

"Thank you for being happy for us. I'll give Toni your endorsement."

~ ~ ~

Candlelight glowed in the dining room as I set the table and tended to dinner. Soft music drifted in from the iPod docked in the living room.

My stomach gurgled, from nervousness rather than hunger, and I hoped I had made the right choice. What I hadn't shared with Bryce was that I had changed my mind back and forth several times, and my waking hours were filled with indecision.

I was sipping a glass of wine when I heard Toni's car door slam, and I walked to the glass French doors in the kitchen to meet her. She smiled brightly when she saw me waiting, and when I opened the door for her to come inside, she kissed me quickly and set her things down near the door.

"I saw your car in the driveway and wondered why you were home so early. I usually make it home before you, even when I'm late."

I clasped her hand and led her into the dining room, where the flickering candlelight created the ambience I wanted.

She took in the table settings, the chilling wine, and the candlelight. "What's this?"

"I've made a special dinner for us to celebrate my decision."

Toni looked at me expectantly. "So, it's good news?" She could barely restrain her excitement. "At least I'm assuming you didn't plan a celebration dinner to tell me, 'Toni, no babies for us.' Correct?" Her smile could have lit up the room.

Butterflies fluttered in my stomach as I took her into my arms. "Oh, we're talking babies, plural, are we? Well, for the time being, I'm only agreeing to one."

She held me tightly. "You've made me so happy!"

I tried to feel the same happiness, but I kept coming back to the nagging doubt in the very depths of my being.

~ ~ ~

As the months flew by, we got more detailed in our family planning. On the surface, I appeared nearly as excited as Toni was, but deep down inside I was terrified, to an extent that not even I knew. I found that I could express happiness over the prospect of having a child because none of it seemed real. It was easy to plan an event that I believed would never come to fruition.

As Toni read books and did research to facilitate her impending motherhood, I busied myself at the studio. The number of our advertising accounts was at an all-time high, and I put Bryce in charge of the interviews for a full time designer to help us with our mounting volume of projects.

I met two of his frontrunners, and decided to hire Ricki Parker, whose portfolio impressed me far more than any of her competition for the job.

~ ~ ~

Ricki gripped my outstretched hand and beamed. "I'm very much looking forward to working here."

It was her first day at the studio, only our second meeting, but I instantly saw why Bryce had described her to me as "sunshine and exuberance." Energy surged from her every pore, and her attractive blonde looks were like a California postcard come to life. Taking an instant liking to her, and applauding Bryce's decision, I welcomed Ricki on board.

Toward the end of the first day, after Ricki had been shown the ropes, I met with Bryce in my office. "Where did you find her?"

"Do I know how to pick 'em?" he boasted.

"She's great. I barely had to give her any direction at all, and she has an energy level that exceeds all of ours put together."

Not much later, as everyone gradually filed out of the office for the evening, Ricki stopped by my office door, briefcase in hand.

"Have a nice evening," she said to us.

"How was day number one?" Bryce asked.

"It was wonderful. I think I'm really going to like it here." She smiled and turned to leave, but before she did, she glanced in my direction, and there seemed to be an added sparkle in her eye as she added, "See you in the morning."

If Bryce noticed a change in Ricki's expression, he didn't mention it. "I'd better be off too, and so should you. Get home to Toni and get started on that family of yours." He chuckled.

"Yeah, yeah. Who's the boss around here anyway?" I teased, but packed my things nevertheless and followed him out the door a few minutes later.

Chapter Fifteen

Toni had taken my decision in favor of parenthood as a signal to move along full speed ahead, and we seemed to disagree at every avenue. I felt that we should be selective about telling people of our plans. Instead, she told friends, family, and coworkers that we were planning a family. I became resentful of her use of the term, and accused her of not considering us a family already.

I grumbled constantly about the parenting books and magazines Toni would leave lying about the house. Everywhere I looked — on the coffee table, on her bedside table — there would be a publication with a baby's smiling face looking up at me.

I allowed all of my frustrations and fears to build up to the point that they more and more frequently escalated into a fight. Our arguments, which had previously consisted of moderate quarrels and resulted in our making up almost immediately, now started out as minor complaints and almost always ended with us not speaking for a good portion of the day.

Toni attributed the increased frequency and anger level of our fights to the stress we were both feeling. I blamed them on the fact that I was feeling neglected for a baby that didn't yet exist and the resentment that was building inside of me.

Even with all the increased tension between us, neither Toni nor I saw what was happening between us for what it really was: a significant crack in our relationship.

~ ~ ~

After a rough winter, Spring arrived again, and I sat with Laurel on the front step of her house, basking in the warm sunlight, feeling my winter pallor slowly turning to a rich bronze. I stretched my legs and breathed deeply, admiring the blooming trees and shrubs coming to life in my favorite season.

Will had taken the girls with him to pick up fast food, Toni was having her car washed and would arrive at any time, and Bryce and his current flame were about to show up for our continuing monthly get-together. Laura and I were sitting in companionable silence, sipping iced tea from oversized tumblers, when suddenly she brought up our plans to have a child.

"How's the baby making coming along?"

I grunted a response. I didn't want to discuss the matter and spoil my weather induced good humor. But it was no use trying to keep anything from my oldest friend.

"No matter what you say, you don't want to have a child, do you?" she surmised.

"I don't want to talk about it," I grumbled.

"Hmm. So how far has the process gone?" she continued, ignoring my reluctance.

I knew that it was no use trying to keep my apprehension from her. "About as far as it can without actual conception, I guess. Toni's changed her diet, and she's been exercising regularly to get her body ready to 'carry the baby,' as she says. I guess it's inevitable now. We have an appointment to review donors next week."

Although I wouldn't meet Laurel's gaze, I knew she was watching me closely. I swallowed the last of my tea with a loud gulp.

"Now what?"

I sorted through my thoughts for a moment before answering. "I don't really understand it myself. I think I'm afraid of the responsibility connected with having a child. I can have a great time with Becca and Kira, but I leave them after an hour or two. This will be twenty-four hours a day, nonstop for the next eighteen years."

Laurel nodded. "Tell me about it."

"I'm being selfish, I know. I don't want to share Toni with anyone. I like having her undivided attention."

Laurel didn't comment; she just continued watching me.

"I'm scared, Laurel." I turned to her, tears suddenly clouding my vision. "This parenting thing is starting to come between us. We argue so much. We never had a serious fight in the first few years we were together, but now we get into it over the most mundane things. What scares me the most is that I'm convinced that Toni would have gone through with this no matter what my answer was. I know that Toni won't want to hear that I may not want to do this. She'll think...okay, she'll *know* I'm being self-centered, and she'll resent my not being as enthusiastic as she is."

Toni pulled up in her newly washed car and waved a greeting.

"I love her more than I've ever loved anyone, Laurel," I said softly as I wiped the tears from my eyes.

"Talk to Toni. Maybe you guys should get some counseling."

I shrugged nonchalantly; I couldn't acknowledge the fear her comment had produced. I rose from my perch on the step and went to meet Toni.

"Hiya, babe." She gave me a quick kiss without seeming to notice that I had been on the verge of tears just a second earlier. "Guess what? I ran into Ricki when I stopped for gas. I invited her over."

I forced a smile. "Great."

Laurel heaved one of her heavy, world-weary sighs and walked into the house, with Toni and me trailing close behind.

An hour later, the seven of us were gathered in Laurel and Will's living room, finishing off the last of take-out Thai food. Kira and Becca, in typical teenager fashion, avoided us and spent most of the evening in their rooms.

As usual, we did more socializing than movie watching. Toni chatted with Laurel while I spoke with Ricki, and Will was deep in conversation with Bryce and his date, Glen.

Ricki was going on about her current project, her eyes dancing as she went into detail. She listed one idea after another for the account. She was, I learned that evening, also deeply interested in interior decorating and landscaping, and had done extensive work on her own home.

"You'll have to come over one day after work and check out my handiwork," she murmured before turning her attention toward the conversation Toni and Laurel were having.

It was the first warning sign I had that I should be cautious in my relationship with Ricki. It was the first of many that I ignored. Her conversation was laced with innuendo, but I refused to acknowledge it at the time. Those words filled my insides with a shaking, fluttering feeling, and not at all an unpleasant feeling.

Late that night, Toni followed me home in her car. I parked my car in our driveway and was gathering my belongings when the passenger door opened and Toni slipped inside and closed the door behind her.

I found her unexpected behavior puzzling. "What are you doing?"

"Shhh," she whispered, her lips inches from mine. "I couldn't wait until we got in the house."

She kissed me then, long and hard. My breathing became rapid and shallow as my hands reached for Toni's hair. My fingers tangled in the thickness of her curls while she skimmed my lips with her tongue.

"Are we going to do this out here?" I inquired breathlessly.

"No." She smiled. "This is just a preview." She hopped out of the car and raced to the front door, expecting me to follow, which I did.

I followed Toni into the dark house and was led upstairs. The instant I stepped through the doorway of our bedroom, she turned to me, her hands everywhere on my body — in my hair, on my face, inside my shirt and along my bare sides. Her mouth met mine hungrily, her sighs and breaths mixed with my own.

She led me to the bed, where we lay atop the sheets touching, kissing, and exchanging words of love. "Promise me forever," she said into my ear as she lay across my body.

I laughed. "Forever, I promise."

Toni took my hand and kissed my palm. "Seriously. Don't play with me. I want this with you forever."

I took her face into my hands and peered to see her face in the blackness of the room. "All right, seriously. I promise you forever." I felt her lips turn up in a smile as she kissed me again, harder.

Chapter Sixteen

Over the following weeks, I immersed myself in my responsibilities at the studio. Toni's attention was focused on areas other than our relationship, as well. Toward the end of the spring semester, her hours at school were increased and her spare time seemed to be filled with learning all she could about motherhood and pregnancy.

One evening toward the end of the week, I arrived home in a sour mood. Things at the office hadn't gone well all week. A brochure for one client was delayed at the printer, another had extensive blueline changes, and yet another client was not satisfied with any of our proposed website designs.

I entered through the back door of the house, and was immediately confronted with dirty dishes in the sink and on the kitchen counter. As I set about putting them in the dishwasher, I recognized the coffee cup I'd used that morning and our dinner dishes from the previous evening.

I slipped off my shoes and moved wearily into the living room, where a coffee table full of magazines caught my eye. Angry, I scooped them up and, without straightening the mess, dumped them unceremoniously into the magazine rack. The last of my patience gone, I stormed upstairs to change clothes.

Shoes in hand, I stomped into the bedroom and found Toni sitting on the bed with the phone cradled between her ear and shoulder. The smile she directed at me when I walked into the room faded when she saw the scowl clouding my face.

I went into the walk-in closet to deposit my shoes on the rack and was changing into jeans when I heard Toni hang up the phone.

"Who was that?" I asked when I stepped from the closet.

"Laurel. She wants us to come over for dinner tonight."

She watched me as I finished dressing, trying to get a clue as to what was causing my black mood. Eventually, she gave up and just asked. "Beth, what's wrong?"

I sighed deeply and turned to face her. "I get home, and the house is a mess. Would it be too much trouble for you to clean it up a little bit? There are magazines and dirty dishes everywhere."

Toni's mouth hung open, and her brow furrowed in anger. "What a sexist thing to say! You can clean up after yourself just as well as I can." She stood facing me, arms crossed defiantly.

"I didn't mean it that way, and you know it," I replied, getting angrier. "But most of that mess down there is yours. I'm sick of coming home to find the house like that."

"Then clean it up! Why are you holding me responsible? I just got home five minutes before you did."

I had pushed the right buttons, and she was in a rage.

"I've suggested many times that we consider having someone come in once a week because of our busy schedules."

"I spend close to sixty hours a week at the office. You more or less work part time. You have more time to clean up." I walked away, an attempt at closing the subject, but then I had another thought. I spun around and added, "And I'm tired of seeing those fucking baby magazines everywhere. You used to be intelligent enough to read something other than those idiotic hetero magazines!"

That did it.

I had begun by complaining about the cleanliness of the house, and that had made Toni angry, but now I had insulted her intelligence. I could see her eyes blazing before I turned to leave the room. As soon as my back was turned, I heard Toni crossing the room in three loud thuds. She grabbed my arm and spun me around to face her.

"How dare you insinuate that I'm stupid!" She glared into my eyes. "I spent more time in school than you did, and studying subjects a hell of a lot more noble than advertising," she hissed. "I guess you think that because you make more money than I do, and because you tool around town in a Jaguar, your intelligence is superior to mine!"

"You don't seem to mind driving that Jag and spending the money I make, do you?" I retorted.

I could see that she was searching for a comeback of her own, but I forestalled her by saying, "I'm going out. You're on your own for dinner. I'm sure Laurel won't mind providing a shoulder for you to cry on!"

I turned and headed down the steps, praying my keys would be downstairs so I wouldn't have to face Toni again. I found them on the kitchen counter and slammed the door behind me when I left.

It was just before seven. I drove around town, trying to calm down before stopping in a restaurant downtown for dinner. I considered calling Bryce and asking him to join me, but decided I wanted to be alone.

After dinner, I was still fuming. I didn't know if Toni had gone to Laurel's or not, but I was afraid of running into her if I went home, so I headed to a nearby bar instead.

I spent several hours downing nothing but club sodas at the bar while watching the other patrons and wondering what problems had brought them here. I replayed the fight over and over in my head, and now that my anger had cooled, I cringed over the awful things I'd said to Toni. I baited her with cruel words, and then went on to pick a full-blown fight.

I paid my tab and walked to my car, trying to think of a place I could find a bouquet of flowers at such a late hour.

By the time I pulled into our driveway, it was nearly eleven. I noticed Toni's car in the driveway and a few dim lights on in the house. I entered through the kitchen, flowers in hand, and searched under the sink for a vase. When I opened the door to our room, I found Toni asleep in the bed. She had left the bedside light on its dimmest setting. I walked to her side of the bed and placed the vase on her bedside table, where the baby magazines had been cleared away. I arranged the flowers and then looked down at her, and was surprised to find her eyes open, watching me.

"Hi."

"Hi," she replied.

"The flowers are from the supermarket. It was the only place still open," I said with an apologetic shrug. She smiled faintly, and I knelt beside her.

"Toni, I'm sorry. I had a horrible day at the office, and I took it out on you." She took my hand. "I never meant to imply that you're not intelligent. You're the smartest woman I know."

Her smile grew as she moved a strand of my hair away from my face. "I'm sorry too. I said some terrible things to you as well." She continued to smile, but underneath the smile, she looked sad and tired. "Come to bed," she whispered.

I rose and removed my clothes, then climbed into bed, where I lay awake for what seemed like half the night, plagued by the increasing number and severity of quarrels we'd been having.

Chapter Seventeen

The first indication that my working relationship with Ricki was heading in an off-limits direction came not too long after that argument with Toni.

Ricki had been increasingly friendly toward me, almost from day one. Before too long, her friendliness turned to flirtation. Why I allowed her to carry on the way she did, I had no idea at the time. I suppose it was because I was so distraught over the situation with Toni wanting us to be mothers, as well as the fact that the attention from Ricki was the only attention I felt I was getting. Ricki had offered smiles directed at only me, as well as little pats on my arm as she spoke, and all with discretion.

Ricki's intentions became crystal clear one evening while I was working late in the office. She had been finishing up a brochure for a meeting the next morning and came into the room, stretching her arms above her head.

"I'm calling it a night," she said with a yawn. "That thing's as close to ready as it will ever be."

I nodded and watched her silently, her recent behaviors making me cautious.

"I thought maybe you'd like to go out for a drink with me," she suggested. I opened my mouth, still searching for an answer. "You're almost finished, aren't you?"

"Yes, but I need to get home."

"Oh, come on. Loosen up." She had her palms flat on my desk, and was leaning toward me provocatively. "Let's have some fun," she murmured. "I won't tell anyone."

I took a deep, ragged breath. My palms were sweating as I laid my pen on the desk. I don't know what drove me to dive into this conversation head on. "What kind of fun are you talking about, Ricki?" My tone was stern, but I was enjoying the banter, basking in the warmth it created in my stomach.

She spun around to sit on the edge of the desk, and doing so wafted the scent of her perfume past me. "I'm up for anything you are," she said.

I was certain she meant more than a couple of drinks between friends. Thankfully I grabbed hold of the first sensible thought in my head and declined. "I can't. You know I'm with someone."

"Hmm." She sighed, rose from her perch, and shuffled toward the door. "Just thought I'd ask. Maybe next time?" She smiled again, grabbed her portfolio case, and disappeared out into the common room, leaving a soft cloud of fragrance behind.

I went home that evening and didn't say a word to Toni about what had happened at the studio. Had I been thinking lucidly, that alone should have alerted me to the fact that there was a problem with my relationship with Toni. I had never kept anything from her before. My discretion wasn't because I didn't want to upset Toni. I kept the incident to myself because I knew that if I shared it with Toni, my flirtation with Ricki would have to be brought to an end, once and for all.

The next morning, my vision was clear enough to see that I was headed toward disaster. Before leaving for the studio, I sat sipping strong coffee at a small patio table outside our house. Toni joined me, dressed for work and towel drying her hair. She had taken the day off, and she had decided to spend these early hours in one of her favorite ways — soaking up the sun's warm rays.

I had decided to finally speak with Toni about my apprehension about becoming a parent, as well as the incident with Ricki, but before I could work up the nerve to begin the conversation, Toni sat beside me and took my hand.

"I've made a decision."

She looked so beautiful. The sun burned deep bronze highlights into her hair, and her smile illuminated her entire face. My heart fluttered as I thought about what I should tell her. How could I consider acting on the desire I felt for Ricki when this wonderful, gorgeous woman was all mine?

"What's simmering in that head of yours?" I teased.

She sipped her coffee and peered over the rim of the mug, the way I had seen her do countless times before.

"Summer isn't too far off, and I think that would be the best time to begin insemination." My smile faded before she could finish. "It would be perfect. I'll have the time to focus on this full speed ahead!"

"That's great," I managed to croak.

She must have noticed the change in emotion on my face, because suddenly she appeared concerned. "What's wrong?"

I placed my mug on the table and stood up. "Nothing." I managed a weak smile. "I just remembered a meeting I have this morning, and I have a few things I need to prepare."

I kissed the top of her head and moved quickly toward the car, wanting to get away before my angry thoughts could spill out in even angrier words.

Chapter Eighteen

My thirty-eighth birthday fell on a warm Saturday in early summer. Toni had planned on taking me out for a celebratory dinner, and since all of our friends wanted to participate in the celebration, we agreed to meet at a local gay bar, Encounters.

We began with a quiet dinner together, enjoying each other's company and conversation. Sipping champagne, we laughed more giddily as the bottle emptied until the inevitable topic of parenthood came up. My mood soured when Toni mentioned our impending motherhood.

She began by saying, "Just think, by your next birthday, we may be parents."

She looked so beautiful sitting across the candlelit table, every dark hair in place, her smile brilliant. My heart expanded within my chest. I realized I was grimacing, and I tried to hide my reaction by lifting the champagne glass to my lips.

"Something wrong?" Toni asked, her smile fading.

"No, nothing," I sputtered unconvincingly. My ability to sidestep convincingly must have been diminished by the champagne, because Toni wasn't buying my lie.

"I notice that whenever I bring up having a baby, you either clam up or suddenly have to run off to the office," she said firmly. "Why won't you talk to me? I've been waiting patiently."

So she hadn't been completely unaware of my feelings all these weeks; she had just been waiting for me to make the first move. I was taken aback by the fact that she knew my level of enthusiasm was less than hers. This time, I had enough alcohol in my system to speak my mind. I drained my glass and set it on the table, averting my eyes so I wouldn't see the disappointment in hers.

"Okay, fine." I began. "I'm unsure about all this. You've been doing all of this planning without much input from me, and I'm not even sure if I want a baby." I let out a sharp breath and still wouldn't look at her. I filled my glass and raised it to my lips, peeking tentatively through the crystal of the goblet to gauge Toni's reaction. She was staring at me stonily, but I was too drunk to stop.

"I don't think I want to share you with someone, and I'm too involved in my career to make time for someone new in my life, someone who will totally depend on me for who knows how many years."

I could see that Toni was hurt, but I was on a roll, finally releasing the flow of words I had been holding in for months. "I don't need another commitment in my life."

That did it.

The second the words left my mouth, a storm cloud formed over us. Toni's demeanor changed from understanding to furious. Her brow furrowed as she hissed, "Oh, is that what I am? An unwanted commitment? And having a child with me would just weigh you down that much more!" She motioned for the check.

"Toni, you're putting words in my mouth!"

"If I'm putting words in your mouth, it's only because you haven't spoken them yourself before now. Dammit, Beth, during all these months of planning, why haven't you said anything? Why did you have to drink half a bottle of champagne before you could talk to me? After all these years together, you don't think you can talk to me?"

I opened my mouth, but the waiter appeared with the check, picked up the credit card Toni had placed on the table, and retreated quickly.

"Baby, I'm sorry," I muttered in a near whisper, but I knew this would take a lot more fixing than just an apology.

The waiter returned with our receipt, which Toni signed. She stood and hurriedly left the restaurant.

Feeling that if I lagged behind, she wouldn't wait for me, I quickly followed Toni to the car. I climbed into the passenger's seat a second after she slid behind the wheel. When I glanced at her, I realized that I'd never seen her look so angry.

"Toni, this is exactly why I didn't speak up. I didn't want you to have this kind of reaction."

She looked into the side view mirror and then pulled out. "We'll talk about this later," she said dismissively.

I wanted nothing more than for us to go home and work this out, but all our friends were waiting to celebrate my birthday, so I sat quietly and let Toni concentrate on getting us safely to the bar.

After a ten minute drive that felt like an hour, Toni parked her car in the club parking lot and got out without a word to me. I knew that it would do me no good to try to repair any damage I'd done until she'd had a chance to cool off, so I followed her into the bar with the good intention of pretending to enjoy what was left of my birthday.

Inside the dimly lit bar, we made our way to the table where Laurel and Will were sitting, along with Kristy and her husband. Toni displayed acting abilities I didn't know she had, as she smiled and greeted everyone cheerily. Not being as talented as she, I uttered a few quick hellos and headed to the bar for drinks. When I returned, Toni was seated and laughing along with all of our friends.

"Where's Bryce?" I managed to ask without sounding as unhappy as I was.

"He's picking Glen up. They should be here soon," Kristy answered. "Ricki's coming too."

I topped off everyone's beers with the pitcher I held in one hand, and I downed a shot of tequila with the other. Sitting next to Toni, I halfheartedly listened to the conversations around me, wanting to be anywhere but there.

Laurel tried to draw me into her conversation with Toni, and I prayed that she wouldn't bring up the baby. I nodded and gave one-word answers to the few questions Laurel directed at me. When I spoke, Toni scanned the dance floor, refusing to turn even the slightest gaze in my direction.

Knowing us both as well as she did, Laurel assessed the situation quickly and rose from her chair. She stood behind me and placed her hands on my shoulders. "Come on, birthday girl.

It's time to replenish drinks."

I dreaded the interrogation I was sure to receive, but knowing that the alternative was sitting there stonily with Toni, I joined Laurel. We walked to the bar, where she ordered another pitcher of beer before turning to me.

"What's up with you two?"

"I told Toni how I feel about having a baby," I muttered. "Over my very special, romantic birthday dinner," I added bitterly.

Laurel sighed as she tried to read my expression. "She's pretty upset, by the looks of it," she ventured.

"Well," I sighed, "I'm afraid I didn't exactly choose the right words to tell her."

Laurel picked up the pitcher and paid the bartender. I mentally thanked the bartender for interrupting our conversation, which allowed Laurel time to choose her next words carefully.

"I told you to talk to her before this got too far, Beth," she said in her tone of motherly reprimand.

"I know. She just made me so angry. And I had a little too much to drink. We'll fix this when we get home."

Looking at me as if I didn't realize the enormity of the situation, Laurel placed her hand on the small of my back to steer me back to our table. "I still think you should consider talking to someone, like a therapist. This is a significant issue that's coming between you."

We arrived at the table, and I resumed my place next to Toni, who was now deep in conversation with Kristy.

By the time Bryce arrived with Glen, and Ricki arrived alone, I'd had quite a few more drinks and was beginning to forget, at least temporarily, the fight that had occurred during dinner. It wasn't long before Ricki, who was seated next to me, noticed that Toni was not paying me any attention.

She leaned closer and whispered, "If your girlfriend isn't going to dance with you on your birthday, I will. Come on." She grabbed my hand and headed for the cramped dance floor. Ricki moved to the blaring music while I stood and watched. "Come on!" she prodded. "Dance with me!"

"Ricki, I'm drunk. I'm going to go sit down."

But just then, a slow number began, and Ricki pulled me into her arms. "Don't worry, I'll hold you up."

Lacking the energy to put up a fight, I gave up and swayed in her arms.

After a few moments, she spoke into my ear. "What's going on with you and Toni?"

"What do you mean?" I stalled.

"She hasn't looked at you or spoken to you since I got here. Considering that you're the guest of honor, it seems sort of strange. What happened?"

I weighed my options. I could walk away and go back to the table, or I could tell her. I glanced at the table and decided it was too far to wobble alone in my condition.

"We had a horrible fight before we got here," I admitted.

Ricki wanted details, but I told her that I didn't want to discuss it. She settled for my answer and pulled me closer, her hand resting low on my back.

When we returned to the table, Toni acknowledged my presence for the first time since we had arrived.

"I think you've had enough to drink," she murmured softly, not meeting my drunken gaze.

She hadn't said it out of concern for me. I could tell she was nowhere near finished being angry. Her concern stemmed from the fact that she'd seen Ricki clutching me during our spin on the dance floor, and she might have felt that the alcohol I'd ingested was disintegrating my ability to be faithful. Unfortunately, she was right.

As the night wore on, instead of celebrating, I became increasingly upset over the situation with Toni. Everyone at our table was drinking, talking, and eating, and Toni hadn't spoken to me since her remark about my alcohol intake. Her rebuke hadn't stopped me, and I remained a bit more than pleasantly tipsy. Glen and Bryce spent much of the time on the dance floor, Kristy and Allen had called it an early night, and Toni was engrossed in conversation with Laurel and Will.

I glanced around the bar and saw that Ricki was talking to a couple seated on bar stools. I stood up to make my way to the ladies room. When I caught Ricki's attention halfway there, I smiled weakly in an attempt to let her know that she was having a better time than I was. I walked into the restroom, which was empty, and stood before a sink. Looking into the mirror above, I saw a tired face looking back at me. I ran some cold water and lowered my face to the basin. As I scooped the cool water into my hands to splash on my face, the door squeaked open and then quietly closed. I looked up to find

Ricki standing behind me, watching my reflection.

She smiled at me and leaned back against the door. "You look like you've had better birthdays," she sympathized.

I laughed and nodded my fuzzy head. "I've been to funerals that were more fun than this get-together." I threw the water from my cupped hands onto my face. The frigid temperature made me gasp, and when I looked up, Ricki was standing next to me, holding a paper towel in her outstretched hand. I accepted it and patted my face and hands dry. She took it from me, tossed it into a waste can, and then took my hand into hers.

"Follow me," she said.

My spinning brain didn't think to decline, and I followed her into the furthest stall and stepped inside. Ricki bolted the door behind me. "What are we doing?" I asked when she faced me.

She moved closer and took my face in her hands. "Happy birthday," she whispered, moving closer. I smelled the alcohol on her breath before I tasted it on her lips. She kissed me so thoroughly, it took me only an instant to respond.

My mind was focused on nothing but the kiss. The liquor I'd had all night long blurred any thoughts I might have had about Toni, or fidelity.

Ricki's kisses turned more forceful, her tongue exploring my mouth while she pulled my shirt from the waistband of my pants and ran her hands across the bare skin.

I moaned softly as she pressed me against the stall door and opened my pants. Before I could protest, her hand was underneath the material and she was sliding her fingers against my wet skin. When I gasped, she broke the kiss.

"Shhh," she whispered with a laugh. "Don't forget this is a public place." She pressed harder against me. "God, I've wanted to do this since the first time I met you." Her lips again found mine.

"No. Ricki, no! I can't do this. I don't want to do this." I struggled to pull her hand from my jeans. "Stop!" I finally disengaged her hand from between my legs and pushed her away from me.

Despite her inebriation, her eyes were large circles. "But—"

"No, Ricki. I'm with Toni. I can't do this." I held my hand between us, worried she might try to come at me again, and even more worried that I might not be strong enough to stop her a second time.

"Here, let me," she offered, helping to close my pants and straighten my shirt.

"Stop. I'm fine. I can do this." I turned my back to her in the tight stall and adjusted my clothing with shaking hands. My disoriented condition increased the difficulty of buttoning my pants, and I could feel Ricki's breath on my neck while she waited. At least she had the decency not to try to touch me again.

"Come on, we'd better get back before they miss us." I unbolted the door, stepped outside the stall, and suddenly felt disoriented under the bright lights, which were sobering me up a bit.

Feeling sick over what had almost happened, and wanting to get far away from Ricki as quickly as I could, I raced for the door. As I reached for the handle, something at the sink caught my eye, and I turned to find Toni watching me, her eyes filling with tears. I murmured her name as her eyes went from me to Ricki.

"Toni, it's not what you think. I—"

"Don't make it worse. I heard you," she said harshly.

My breath was coming in short, shallow puffs, and my face burned. I fumbled for something to say, something to make the heartbroken look on her face disappear, but I couldn't think of anything.

"I can't believe you did this," she sobbed, then she twisted the door handle and rushed outside.

I moved to follow her, but a sudden wave of nausea twisted my insides. I turned and pushed Ricki aside, then hurried into the nearest stall. I barely made it before I heaved, undoubtedly from both guilt and the alcohol. I heaved until my stomach was empty. I rocked back on my heels, trying to regain my bearings, wiping the sweat from my face with the back of my hand.

"Here, let me help you."

Ricki was behind me, pulling my hair away from my face. I stood up slowly, holding on to the sides of the stall for support.

"Ricki," I ground out between clenched teeth, "please leave me alone. We've done enough damage for one evening."

She backed away from me as I made my way to the sink and rinsed my mouth with the cool water. I turned and glanced at her one last time before leaving the restroom, and then I moved back to the table as quickly as my impaired balance would allow. Everyone sat there staring at me in shock. Everyone but

Toni.

I was panicked, and hot tears coursed down my cheeks. "Where is she? Where's Toni?" I wailed.

"She left. She was crying," Laurel answered. "God, Beth, what the hell happened?"

"Take me home. Would somebody take me home, please?"

I grabbed my purse and waited as Laurel and Will gathered their things. I happened to glance at Bryce just as he saw Ricki walking out of the ladies room. His face said all I needed to know. He assumed, correctly, what had happened. I led the way outside without another word.

The ride to the house was agonizingly long. I sobbed the entire way, while Laurel, turned sideways in the front seat, tried to get me to tell them what had happened.

"I need to talk to Toni, make her understand" I sobbed.

"Why? What happened back there?" Laurel asked.

I knew I was scaring her, so I took a few deep breaths and blew my nose before trying to explain. "Ricki and I were in the bathroom together, and Toni walked in on us."

"She found you kissing?" Laurel was incredulous.

I shook my head. "More."

"What!" she blurted. "Please tell me you weren't having sex with Ricki!"

I groaned. My stomach threatened another uprising.

She was outraged. "What the hell is wrong with you?"

"It's not what you think, Laurel. It... I stopped Ricki before it came to that. She touched me, and...I stopped her, but Toni thinks more happened."

"What the hell were you even doing in there with another woman?" Will tried to soothe her, but Laurel brushed him off and continued her tirade.

Thankfully, we arrived at our house before Laurel could get much further in her scathing reprimand. Will pulled in next to Toni's parked car. The lights were blazing inside.

Will turned off the engine and turned to face me. "We'll wait here," he said.

"You can leave. Thanks for the ride." I was almost out the door when he said something that turned my blood cold.

"She may not let you stay. We'll wait here."

Without replying, I got out of the car and hurried to the front door.

The evening air cooled my skin, but once I was in the house with the door shut behind me, the stuffiness raised a sweat. I nervously searched from room to room, not finding Toni, although lights were burning in each room I entered. I heard a noise coming from our bedroom upstairs. Chewing on my nails, something I hadn't done since college, I climbed the stairs.

I stepped into the room and saw a suitcase lying open on our bed. My heart fell, and I suddenly felt nauseous again. I heard hangers clattering in the walk-in closet before I saw Toni walking out, her hands full of my clothes. She stopped when she saw me, and we watched each other warily from across the room.

"I'm so sorry, Toni."

She shook her head angrily, and dropped my clothes into the open suitcase before she collapsed onto the bed. My heart broke as she sat crying, her face in her hands. I started to move toward her, but she looked up quickly.

"Stop. Don't come near me." Her eyes were swollen, and she used the heel of her hand to wipe away the fresh tears.

I stopped where I was and knelt on the floor, just feet away from the bed. "You've got to let me explain. That wasn't me—"

She laughed bitterly. "Who was it then? Christ, Beth, give me a break. I heard you! I heard you fucking her!" She broke into fresh sobs.

I stayed where I was, but reached out to touch her. "No. No, you're wrong, Toni. I didn't touch her, I swear. I did *nothing* to her, and she means *nothing* to me. I would never... Baby," I pleaded, "let me explain what happened."

She pushed my hand away. "Give me a fucking break. Do you think that letting her fuck you but you doing nothing to her in return makes it any better? Stop hiding behind logistics, you were unfaithful, Beth. How long have you been fucking her?"

"I'm not...we're not... It's not like that, Toni. Tonight just happened. I was drinking too much and—"

"Don't blame it on the drinking. It's more than that! God, you're no better than Rebecca! I never thought you would do what she did." She stood up from the bed and slammed the suitcase. "I won't put up with this like I did with her. I want you out of here."

She picked up the bag and headed down the stairs before I could stop her. I scrambled from the floor and followed her to the front door, where she stood holding the suitcase. I was crying so hard that I wasn't sure she'd be able to understand me, but I had to try.

"Please don't make me leave. Nothing happened, Toni. I didn't touch her!" I sat down on the bottom step, and Toni slammed the suitcase down. She was still crying, but she was more furious than anything else.

"You don't get it, do you, Beth? You've broken my trust. You've betrayed me and our life together. And you did it just as we were planning a family. How am I supposed to forgive that? No. I can't. I won't. Get out!" she screamed.

In all the years we had been together, neither Toni nor I had raised our voices to each other, not even during any of the bitter arguments we'd been having recently, and here she was screaming for me to leave.

I shook my head and wailed, "No!"

"God damn it, Beth! Get the fuck out of this house! You're no better than any other woman I've ever dated. I just can't believe it took me so many years to figure you out!"

The door opened, and Laurel and Will gingerly stepped inside. Apparently Toni's initial shouting had alerted them that their intervention might be needed.

Toni leaned against a wall, breathing deeply, trying to control herself. She looked at our friends and pleaded, "Get her out of here, please. I've never been this angry in my life, and I'm afraid I might hurt her."

Laurel and Will stood stock still, neither seeming to comprehend.

I could see that Toni's hands were shaking, and she seemed close to hyperventilating.

"I swear," she held her hand up with her forefinger and thumb less than an inch apart, "I'm this close to hitting her, and I don't want to do that. Please take her home with you. Please." She broke into a fresh crying jag as she turned and walked toward the living room, Laurel following her.

Will walked over to me, crouched down to my level, and held my hands. "You okay, honey?" he asked.

I sniffed and shook my head.

He brushed my hair from my face and said soothingly, "We'd better get you out of here."

When he saw that I had no intention of budging, he added, "You've got to give her some time to calm down, sweetie. You can't stay here tonight."

I nodded, and he helped me stand. I glanced toward the living room on my way out and saw Toni sitting with Laurel. Toni looked up at me just once, and I saw no love in her face whatsoever, just pain and anger.

Will called to Laurel that he'd be waiting with me in the car, then he led me outside.

In the car, we waited in silence for Laurel, who was undoubtedly trying to calm Toni before she joined us. When she finally came out to the car, she glanced at me through the window, and I could see that she was crying too.

Chapter Nineteen

The sun blazed through the window of Will and Laurel's guestroom, and I woke up gasping from the stifling heat of the room. I scrambled out of the springy bed, heedless of my aching back, and went to the window to let some air in before falling back into bed to rest my pounding head. It took me only a second to remember what had happened the night before, and I wrapped a pillow around my head in an attempt to smother the memories. I had come directly to bed and lay awake crying until my eyes burned and itched, but sleep hadn't come for hours.

Since it was Sunday, I expected to hear the kids running about, but I heard nothing. Realizing that the pillow I'd crammed my head into wouldn't erase my painful memories, I crawled out of bed and trudged downstairs. I found Laurel alone, reading the paper. She appeared so calm, I almost let myself believe that I had imagined why I was there, until she looked up from her paper and I saw that her eyes looked as tired as mine felt.

She set the newspaper on the armrest of the sofa and patted the cushion next to her.

"You look horrible. Did you get any sleep?" Her concern was evident in her voice. I was so relieved that she was speaking to me, I almost began crying again.

"A little," I croaked. "Do you hate me, too?"

She reached over and hugged me. "Of course not."

I let out the breath I had been holding. "Where is everyone?"

"I asked Will to take the girls out so we could talk. I didn't think you'd want them seeing you like this."

I nodded. "I've really messed up this time, Laurel. I don't know what I was thinking." When Laurel didn't reply, I continued, "I've never seen Toni like she was last night. She hates me."

"She doesn't hate you, she's just hurt." Laurel's attempt to reassure me was not very convincing. "I called her this morning to see how she is, because she scared me last night too. She asked me to tell you not to call her today. She's had a rough night, and she's not up to talking about this." Laurel saw the disappointment on my face. "She's not going to work tomorrow, so maybe you can talk then."

I had hoped to wake up and find a light at the end of the tunnel, but what Laurel had said wasn't helping. "I'm so scared. I never stopped to think that I might lose her." I could feel the hot tears burning their way down my cheeks, the same path they had taken last night.

"I'm sorry for the way I reacted last night," Laurel offered, and then held me while I cried on her shoulder. We stayed that way for several minutes. "You want to tell me what happened?" she asked once my breathing was regular again.

I went through every sordid bit of it, included more details of our confrontation over dinner.

"So Toni knew all along you were upset about her wanting to get pregnant?"

"From what she said at dinner, it sounds like it." I wiped my face with my hand. "We were both unwilling to talk about it, and it all turned out so badly."

Laurel offered to get me something to eat, but I decided to go back upstairs and try to sleep. I thought that maybe if I was asleep, it would keep me from worrying about the terrible mess I'd gotten myself into.

Chapter Twenty

Knowing I wouldn't be of any use in the studio in the condition I was in on Monday, I called Bryce's extension and left a voice-mail, being careful to call before he would be in. I didn't want to face anyone. I spent the morning pacing Laurel's house, trying to build up the courage to call Toni.

At about 8 o'clock, the phone rang.

"Hi, it's me."

Toni's voice sounded calm, which I took as a good omen. "Hi."

There was a moment of dead silence, and then she said, "Would it be all right if I come over there to talk, or are you on your way to the office?"

This time I noticed that she sounded nasal, leading me to believe that she'd been crying. "I'm not going to work," I said timidly.

"Then I'll come right over, if that's okay."

"Uh, sure. I'll see you soon. Bye"

After we hung up, I ran upstairs to brush my hair and teeth, and change into clean clothes. I'd been living in sweats since Saturday night.

Within half an hour, Toni was at the front door. My heart

went out to her. She looked like she hadn't slept in days, and her eyes were red and swollen. I held the door for her, and we went into the living room without a word being spoken. She sat on the sofa, and held out her hand.

"I brought your car. I thought you'd need it."

I reached out and took the keys. In her other hand, she clutched a wad of tissues. I could tell she wasn't expecting our discussion to go well, and since she'd brought me my car, I wasn't either.

"I'm sorry," I began.

She surprised me by answering, "I don't want to talk about it." Her voice was hoarse, and she wouldn't look at me.

"I...I thought you came here so we could talk this out," I stuttered.

She swallowed several times. I could see that she was trying not to cry.

"I want to talk about the house, our agreement," she finally said.

When we purchased the house, Toni and I had an agreement drawn up in the event of a break-up. We agreed that if either of us wanted the house and the other didn't, the interested party would buy the other out. If neither or both of us wanted the house and couldn't work out a settlement, we would sell it. We had planned on waiting six months after the hypothetical break-up before we decided anything. The fact that this was what she wanted to discuss definitely wasn't a good sign.

"What about it?" I could barely get the words out.

"I don't want the house, do you?"

I felt as if someone had punched the air out of my lungs. "Wait, no. Toni, I thought we could try to work this out. I don't want to break up." I concentrated on controlling my breathing.

"I can't be with you after what you did," she whispered. The air was thick with silence until she continued. "I'd like to decide what we're going to do about the house today."

"Why aren't you giving me a chance?" I pleaded. She met my gaze, and I saw anger blazing in her eyes.

"Why should I give you a chance? What kind of chance did you give me? You thought nothing about going into that bathroom with someone else. What chance did I have then? Did you even think about me?"

I was too shocked to respond, but apparently she did not expect an answer.

"Do you know what the worst part is, Beth? It's not even that you fucked her, it's that you did it with me sitting fifty feet away!"

I had a moment to feel miserable about that while she blew her nose.

"I've been so stupid" she began again. "I honestly never thought that we'd break up. All I've ever wanted was to have a relationship as good as my parents have, and you're the only one I've ever had that with. I never believed you'd hurt me. I was wrong."

I wanted to defend myself, but no words would come. I reached out to comfort her, and to my surprise, she let me touch her.

"Toni, please listen." I stroked her hair. "I never meant to hurt you. I made a huge mistake, but it wasn't done to hurt you."

I could see she was watching something outside, and I looked out the picture window to find that a taxi had pulled into the driveway. The taxi driver tapped the horn, and she moved away, out of my reach.

"I'm going away for a week or two. When I come back, I'll look for an apartment, so please let me know by then if you want to keep the house."

Before I could say anything, she was gone — out the door and getting into the taxi, going home to the house that wouldn't be ours anymore.

Chapter Twenty-One

I learned from Laurel that Toni went away to spend time with her parents. It was clear that she wouldn't change her mind about taking me back. I found a modest apartment downtown, just a few blocks from the office, and moved my belongings from the house while Toni was gone. Before moving the last few boxes, I wrote her a short note.

Dear Toni:

I don't want to live in this house without you. If you want to stay, we can make some kind of arrangement. If you really want to sell it, please stay here until it sells. I don't want you to have to leave because of my mistakes.

Beth

I dropped the note, along with my set of keys, into the mail slot, and drove the last of my belongings to my apartment.

Weeks wore on with excruciating slowness, and I found that I worked too much with too little patience. Bryce and Kristy were at their wits end with me, and Ricki quit —partly out of guilt, and partly because Bryce resented her for her part in my break-up with Toni and was relentlessly cruel to her. After that fateful evening, she lasted only two weeks before she came into my office and said she felt it would be best if she left. I didn't put up a fight. I asked Bryce to take on more responsibilities, mainly because I couldn't focus on one thing for very long and obvious mistakes that I'd made were becoming obvious.

I kept to myself most days, even opting to work from home at least two days a week. When I managed to drag myself into the office, I usually closed the door behind me, forcing my staff to use email to communicate with me. I almost never remembered to eat, so my clothes were beginning to hang on me. I was miserable to be around, and I knew it. If I could have opted out of spending time with myself, I would have.

My depression deepened, and I often woke up, dressed, and went to the studio, only to tell my staff that I had to leave. Then I'd drive randomly. Sometimes I would find myself at a park and sit all day, brooding, regretting. Other times, I would drive to Laurel's and lay on the sofa until I knew she and Will would be coming home.

The worst part was that I hadn't seen or spoken to Toni since the day she'd brought my car to me. The only tidbits of information I could get were those that Laurel provided. Yes, she was back from visiting her parents. Yes, she looked a little better, but not much. She'd lost some weight; she was back at work; she was looking for a real estate agent to list the house with. She asked Laurel if she thought I'd want to have a hand in choosing the agent. Laurel told her she didn't think so.

Although I constantly asked Laurel how Toni was doing, Laurel never indicated that Toni was asking about me. When the house was put on the market, I heard it from the realtor, who called to make an appointment with me to sign the necessary paperwork. I never once heard from Toni.

Laurel was concerned about my losing weight. I knew I was worrying her, so I accepted when she invited me to dinner one evening. Since I showed no enthusiasm for any dish Laurel suggested, she thought it would be a good idea for us to go to my favorite health food store to get some ideas.

Once there, I walked up and down the aisles without much interest in the items on the shelves. Laurel followed me with a cart and chose items indiscriminately.

I wasn't paying attention as I rounded a corner and almost slammed right into Toni. It was almost three months after our break-up. How we managed to avoid each other all that time in such a small town, I didn't know.

The surprise I felt at seeing her was doubled when I saw that a woman was not only standing next to her, but had her arm draped casually around Toni's waist, her fingers locked through a belt loop in Toni's jeans.

We managed an uncomfortable greeting. When Laurel joined us, the relief was evident on Toni's face.

"Laurel, hi!" Her enthusiasm sounded forced. She looked at the woman with her, who was now gripping Toni's belt loop as if it was a lifeline.

"You know Leah, don't you?"

I looked at Laurel, as she was the one to whom Toni had directed the question.

Toni introduced me quickly, probably hoping that I

wouldn't make a scene and that this woman, who seemed to be her new girlfriend, wouldn't figure out who I was. To my amazement, Toni turned to me and asked, "How are you doing?"

Struck speechless by the shock of seeing her with someone else, I could only nod.

I took some satisfaction in the fact that Toni appeared to be as uncomfortable as I was.

"Well," she said, "we've got to run. See you around."

They sped to another aisle as I turned to Laurel. "Who the hell was that?" I whispered angrily.

"She works in the main office at school," Laurel answered sheepishly.

"Why didn't you tell me Toni was seeing someone already?"

"I had no idea. She never said a word to me."

I glared at Laurel, my mind searching for an appropriate punishment for betraying one's best friend.

She must have read my mind. "Don't look at me that way, I'm telling the truth. You saw how uncomfortable she looked. She didn't want me to know about it either."

"What the fuck is with that goddamn school anyway? Sounds like it's chock full of fucking lesbians!" I knew that I sounded childish, and I turned on my heel and headed for the exit.

"Where are you going?" Laurel called after me.

"I'm not hungry anymore."

~ ~ ~

After that incident, the gods decided to twist the knife and have me run into Toni almost each and every time I showed my face in public. It was markedly worse than not seeing her at all.

Soon after our encounter in the store, we ran into each other at the bank. I was at the cash machine. When I finished my transaction, I turned to find Toni standing near the door, watching me.

"Oh!" My surprised exclamation was all I could manage.

She looked good, too good. Every hair was in place, and she was dressed impeccably. She'd probably just come from school.

"Hi," she said softly.

"Hi." I placed my card and cash into my wallet and slipped it into my bag.

At least one on one, we were comfortable enough to exchange words.

"You didn't really answer me the last time we met, but how are you doing?" she asked.

"Um, well...I've been better. How about you?"

My form of communication of the previous week seemed to have been contagious, as she simply nodded.

"Are you still seeing...Leah, is it?" There was more than just a touch of cattiness in my question.

Tension clear in her voice, Toni answered, "Yeah, it's Leah, and yes, I'm still seeing her."

"Hmm, dating a co-worker." It was out of my mouth before I had a chance to realize what I was saying.

"Well, at least she's not my employee," she retorted, eyes glaring, arms crossed. Her body language alone could have maimed me.

Instantly regretful, I said, "I deserved that."

"Yes, you did."

I moved closer to the door, not really wanting to leave but knowing that I had to.

"Look, this is hard on both of us, but it's inevitable that we're going to find ourselves in each other's company from time to time. This is a small town, and we share almost every friend we have." She waited for a response.

"What's your point, Toni?" I wasn't angry, just resigned.

"I just mean..." She stared at her hands nervously. "Well, I want for us to be civil to each other. We'll be thrown into a lot of social situations, and I don't want either of us to be uncomfortable. I don't hate you Beth, I just can't be with you. I hope we can find a way to be friends again someday."

I could feel the tears beginning. I wanted to hold her hands and ask her how things had gone so wrong. I wanted to tell her how much I missed her, and how it was barely worth waking up every day without her next to me. I longed to tell her I still loved her. Instead of all that, I muttered, "I'll try."

She looked up just in time to catch me wiping away a stray tear.

"I need to go now," she said as her turn at the ATM came up, but she stood watching me.

"Yeah, I know. Me too." I knew if I stayed any longer, I would lose what little composure I had and break down completely.

"Take care, Toni," I offered before turning away.

I barely heard her answer, "You too," before her footsteps echoed away.

Chapter Twenty-Two

After my break-up with Toni, Laurel and Will resumed their self-imposed roles of surrogate parents to me, roles they had been sure they were through with when Toni and I met. They worried about me, and with good reason. Not only had I lost significant weight, but my sense of humor was gone, and I despised myself for having destroyed my own happiness. Laurel began insisting that I come for dinner on a weekly basis and I usually accepted, just so her worrying about me would ease up a bit.

One evening after Will and Laurel had watched me not eat yet again, the girls settled at the dining room table to work on their homework and Will offered to clean up while Laurel and I settled on the sofa. We started by talking about our work, which inevitably led me to ask about Toni.

"Do you see her much?" I asked.

Laurel shrugged. "Occasionally."

"We ran into each other at the bank a while ago," I told her, realizing that it had been almost a month.

"I know, she told me. Didn't go too well, did it?"

"I don't know. We tried, I guess." I attempted to sound indifferent. "Is she still dating the woman from your school?"

"I'm not sure, but I think so. I told you before, she doesn't really talk to me about that."

"I wish I could get over her as easily as she did me," I said forlornly, giving Laurel the excuse she needed to lean over and give me a push.

"Stop feeling sorry for yourself. She's not dating because she's over you, she's dating to *get* over you." She laughed.

I looked sideways at her. "How do you know? Did Toni tell you that?"

Laurel stretched and rested her feet on my lap. "What's happening to the world when I have to teach you about women? No, she didn't tell me. It's just obvious it won't last."

I remained doubtful. "Just because it won't last doesn't mean I have a chance."

"Well, I can't answer that, unfortunately."

We were watching television when the phone rang, and I heard Will answer in the kitchen. He muttered a few words before I heard him say, "Yeah, as a matter of fact, she's here. Hold on."

He brought the phone in and handed it to me. "It's Toni," he whispered.

My heart began to race and I looked at Laurel questioningly, but she looked as puzzled as I was.

"Hello?"

"Hi, Beth. I'm sorry to be calling you there, but I've been trying to get in touch with you all night, and I just called there to see if Laurel would know where you are," she said in a rush.

"It's all right" I attempted to sound nonchalant. "What's up?"

"We have an offer on the house."

Shock tore the breath from my lungs. I could hear the line humming. My hands were sweating; my breath returned in short gulps.

When I didn't respond, Toni filled the silence. "I was hoping you'd come over so we could discuss it. I think it sounds like a good offer."

I couldn't speak.

"Beth?" Toni prodded.

I forced myself to answer. "When do you want to do it?"

"Are you free tomorrow?"

We set a time to meet and hung up quickly.

If I hadn't been so miserable, I would have laughed at Will's and Laurel's expressions. They both watched me with their mouths agape, waiting to learn what the phone call was about.

"There's an offer on the house," I said as I handed Will the phone.

They both let out the breath they'd been holding.

I turned to Laurel. "You remember that question you didn't have the answer to? I can answer that for you now if you'd like."

~ ~ ~

I stood outside the front door of the house Toni and I had shared, feeling odd at having to knock. Toni answered immediately, as if she had been waiting right inside the door for me to arrive.

"Hi." She smiled cautiously as she stepped back and let me

in. Her dark hair was pulled back from her face, and she wore a white tee-shirt tucked into faded jeans. She took my breath away, as she always had.

"I want to talk to you before we do this." I knew that this could be my last chance, and I wanted to take advantage of it.

She looked surprised. "Sure, let's sit down."

I sat near her on the sofa and tried to put my thoughts in order. "I want to talk about what happened."

She sighed and sat back on the couch. "All right. What about it?"

Seeing that she was at least willing to listen, I relaxed a bit. "I know I hurt you, and—"

"We hurt each other."

That took me off guard. "What?"

"I realize that now. I've thought a lot about it, and I know now that I hurt you too. I knew you weren't happy with my plans to have a baby, but I ignored your feelings and went forward with my arrangements. I...I was selfish."

I gaped at her for a few seconds. Maybe this would go the way I had hoped.

She noticed my expression and laughed softly. "You look surprised to hear me say that."

I smiled then. It felt like the first time in months, and it probably was. "I am, a little. Toni, I know I hurt you badly, but I miss you and I want for us to work things out."

There! It was out. I took a couple of deep breaths before I realized she wasn't looking at me anymore, she was watching her hands, the way she had been that day at the bank. The way she did when she was uncomfortable.

"Just because I acknowledge my part in our break-up doesn't mean the hurt and mistrust aren't still there," she said quietly.

"I know that. If you give me a second chance, I'll take the hurt away, I promise."

No. She was shaking her head no. This was going all wrong.

"No? What do you mean no? No what?" I knew I sounded desperate.

"Beth, no one has hurt me like you did, because I never loved anyone as much as I loved you. I can't let it happen again."

Loved? Past tense. "It won't happen again!" I promised.

"I don't know that! I don't trust you anymore!"

My mind raced to think of what I could say next to persuade her, but I was too slow. "What's a relationship without trust?" Her voice broke.

"It'll never happen again," I repeated inanely.

"You're right, it won't, because I'm not going to give you that chance."

Her face was turning red, and I could tell she was beginning to get angry.

"Every time I look at you, I remember how you looked coming out of that stall with another woman." She was beginning to cry.

"It was a mistake!" My voice rose. "It was the only time it happened, and I was drunk. And despite what you believe, I didn't have sex with her."

She was again shaking her head. "It shouldn't have happened at all, but it did, and now we're both paying for it."

That was all it took for me to become as angry as she was. "How are you paying for it, Toni? You've already found someone else. Is that what this is about? Are you refusing to give me another chance because you're in love with Leah?" This revelation had just come to me as I spoke.

"Leah has nothing to do with this," Toni answered quickly. "And she's none of your business."

"Well, for someone who says I hurt her so badly, you sure got over it fast enough!

What was it, a month after we broke up that you started seeing her?" I knew I was going too far, but I couldn't stop. Even the steely look in Toni's eyes didn't deter me.

"Stop it," she warned.

"Maybe that's it," I said. She waited for me to continue. "How long were you fucking Leah before you broke up with me?"

Her mouth dropped open. "How dare you!" she fumed. "How dare you turn this around on me! God, you infuriate me!"

I saw that her hands were clenched and shaking, much like they were the night she had pleaded with Laurel and Will to take me home with them.

"Are you going to hit me now that Laurel's not here to stop you?" I asked angrily, with no fear at all. My eyes narrowed, and I said through clenched teeth, "Go ahead, hit me! You've been wanting to for months." I plucked her hand from her lap and tried to swing it at my face. "Come on, hit me!"

She pulled her arm from my grasp and stood up. "I'm not

going to hit you."

Her breathing was coming in short gasps, and she looked like wanted to kill me, not just hit me. "Just sign the papers and get the hell out of here!" she said as I stood up and walked to the door.

"Fuck your papers. I'm not signing anything."

I stormed out of the house, got into my car, and sped out of the driveway. I didn't even care where I was going. After what felt like miles, I pulled over to calm myself. I press my palms to my hot face, and realized I was wiping away tears.

~ ~ ~

The following morning, I crawled out of bed before the sun came up. I had spent a large portion of the previous night crying and thinking. I showered, dressed, and brewed a strong pot of coffee, a tumbler of which I took to the office with me. I closed the door and worked quietly, not even greeting Bryce and Kristy when they came in at nine. I waited patiently until ten o'clock, when I knew Toni would be on her way to work, and then I picked up the phone.

I dialed the number that had been my own for so long. While waiting for the answering machine to pick up, I rubbed my tired eyes and sipped the strong, bitter coffee. When the machine's beep sounded, I began to speak slowly, clearly, and wearily.

"Toni, it's me. Send me the paperwork on the house, and I'll sign it. I'm sure you need it as soon as possible, so I'll have Bryce call you with my Fed Ex account number."

I hesitated before continuing. "I'm sorry about last night. I hope I didn't scare you as much as I scared myself. Take care of yourself." I hung up and downed the dregs of the coffee in my cup.

Chapter Twenty-Three

The paperwork was signed; the house was officially sold. I pretended to get on with my life. Giving up our house was a harsh slap in the face for me. It forced me to realize — without any room for doubt — that my relationship with Toni was over.

I poured myself into my career more frantically than ever, keeping to myself and avoiding getting close to anyone who could hurt me, or who I could hurt. I wasn't even interested in friendships; friendship could lead to other things.

Probably because of my self-imposed exile, Bryce appeared in my doorway on a cold, snowy day after Christmas. Apparently he'd had enough of my seclusion.

He took a seat in the chair facing my desk. "How's it going, boss?"

I looked up from my paperwork. Beneath his smile, Bryce looked concerned. "I'm all right, Bryce," I said automatically. "What's up?"

He smiled engagingly. "Let me take you out to dinner tonight." When I didn't answer, he tried a different approach. "Come on, I'm lonely. I'll take you anywhere you like, and then we'll hit some bars. It's about time we let the world know we're on the market."

I wanted nothing more than to head home after work and go to bed with a book. I shook my head and replied weakly, "I have too much work to catch up on."

"You don't have work to catch up on. That's all you do. You're all caught up on every account we have," he argued.

"Now that you and Glen are no longer an item, you might be ready for bars, Bryce, but I'm not."

"Okay," he leaned over the desk, "no bar. But have dinner with me. You're one of my best friends, and I miss you."

I didn't know if he meant it or if he was trying to sweet-talk me, but it worked. "I'll agree, on one condition. I'm treating. I don't pay you enough for you to take me anywhere decent," I joked. "Now get back to work before I change my mind."

Bryce smiled and rose from the chair, took my hand, and kissed it tenderly. "Thank you for the honor of your company. As for me not being paid enough, we'll talk about that tonight." He grinned mischievously before leaving me to my paperwork.

Although it was a Friday night, I chose a restaurant that was quiet enough for us to make conversation. We sat in a dimly lit corner and talked for the first time in months about something other than work.

"Why have you been shutting yourself off from all of us?" Bryce asked almost immediately.

I was astounded by his frontal assault. "Why would anyone want to be around me? I haven't exactly been the life of the party the last six months."

"That's precisely my point. You're going through a rough time, and you're not letting us help." He reached across the table and patted my hand. "You don't have to be alone, you know."

"I know that, Bryce. I just haven't wanted to bring everyone else down. Where I am is my own doing. I can deal with it on my own." He looked at me doubtfully and sipped his drink.

"Besides," I continued, "if I'm hanging around, how will you pick up men?"

He laughed then, and rolled his eyes. "Oh, don't you worry, honey, I'll manage. And that's a cop-out! You should be getting out there with me and finding someone to take your mind off of Toni."

I shook my head. "I don't want anybody." I regretted agreeing to dinner when I saw the pity in his eyes.

"Is there any chance of you and Toni working things out? I've been wanting to ask, but I didn't want to upset you."

"The last time we spoke was when she put the house up for sale. I created a horrible scene, and she'll probably never forgive me, with good reason. So, unfortunately, the answer to your question is no, no reconciliation possible."

Bryce had listened intently and occasionally nibbled at his meal. "I'm guessing that Laurel keeps you updated on how Toni's doing and what she's up to," he said. "Or am I assuming incorrectly that you want to know?"

"She does, and I do. Laurel doesn't say too much, probably partly out of loyalty to Toni and partly because she doesn't want to pour salt into my wounds by constantly bringing her up."

Bryce stopped mid-bite and looked at me. "I'm sorry, boss. Is that what I'm doing?"

Feeling a sudden rush of love for him, I smiled at him warmly. "No, not at all. It actually feels good to be talking about this."

"Okay then, continue. I feel like I've been out of the loop for too long."

"You're a gossip queen, you know that?" I whispered, throwing a sprig of parsley at him. "Laurel said that Toni's no longer seeing the woman I saw with her at the health food store, and she's going forward with her plans to have a baby."

Bryce's expression showed his astonishment, and I nodded my agreement. "I know, I can't believe it either. I guess I was arrogant enough to think that having a baby was something she'd only consider doing with me."

I detected pity in Bryce's expression again, and changed the subject. "Let's finish up and rent some trashy movies."

He nodded his approval and turned back to his dinner without comment.

Chapter Twenty-Four

Almost eight months to the day after our break-up, Toni and I signed away ownership of our house. The financing for the new owners had been approved, and Toni and I were scheduled to meet them at the title company to sign over the property.

I arrived ten minutes before our appointed time to find Toni already there, along with the realtor. Their conversation came to an abrupt stop when they saw me, and Toni offered me a tentative smile.

The agent shook my hand. "We're just waiting for the buyers." She offered me coffee and went off to fetch it for me when I accepted. Toni and I sat down in the lobby.

Toni looked at me warily, probably unsure as to how she should approach me because of what had occurred the last time we'd been together.

"I won't ask how you are," she began. "This is difficult for me, too."

I found that hard to believe. She looked radiant. Her eyes glistened, which deepened their dark brown color. Her hair even seemed to shine more than usual.

It was evident that neither of us knew what to say to the other. We were both uncomfortable in each other's presence, and I was thankful when the realtor reappeared with my coffee.

"Ah, here they are now," she said, as she spotted the buyers at the door. "We should be able to begin in a moment."

Toni and I were introduced to the young couple, and then we were all whisked into an adjoining office to sign the paperwork. As I walked into the spacious office, I tried not to hate the soon-to-be owners of the house I loved. It wasn't their fault Toni and I had separated; it was mine.

As if from a distance, I watched as page after page was signed or initialed by the couple, and I signed my own name as each page was placed before me. The words of the title company representative were drowned out by the blood rushing through my ears. The room became unbearably hot, and my pulse raced as Toni and I signed away our last tie to each other. My breathing was becoming labored as the last page was signed and checks for the profit from the sale were handed to each of us. The air in the room felt thin entering my lungs. The whole scene appeared to be happening at a distance.

When I was sure I was no longer needed, I rose quickly, excused myself, and left the office, hurrying into the hallway. My hands were shaking uncontrollably, and my heartbeat was rapid. I made it to a chair in the small lobby near the elevators and rested my head in my hands, elbows pressed into my knees. I tried to regain my equilibrium by taking deep, deliberate breaths.

I heard the sound of clicking heels coming closer and looked up to see Toni hurrying toward me, a concerned look on her face.

She knelt before me and took my hand. "Are you all right?"

I attempted a smile, as much to reassure myself as to reassure her. "Panic attack, I think." I could feel my heart returning to its normal rhythm. "I've been having them lately, but this has been the worst one so far."

Toni took a seat near me and frowned. "I'm sorry," she murmured.

When I looked confused, she added, "About everything."

I sat quietly until my breathing returned to normal before asking about her living arrangements.

"I found a townhouse not too far from Laurel's. I wanted something permanent, not just an apartment."

I looked down at my hands, which had ceased shaking, and searched for something to say. I didn't want her to leave. "Laurel tells me that you're trying to get pregnant." When I looked up, a brilliant smile was lighting up her entire face.

"Yeah...well...um..." She cleared her throat and smiled again. God, she was beautiful. "Actually, I haven't told anyone but my parents, but I'm pregnant already. The insemination was successful almost immediately, which is pretty unheard of."

When the words sunk in, I fought to keep my pulse from resuming its erratic tempo.

"Oh." No wonder she looked so radiant, and had glittering eyes and bouncing hair. *Be happy for her*, I told myself. *This is important to her.*

"Congratulations!" I sputtered.

The smile on her face could have lit a city block and part of me felt overjoyed for her. I looked down at the check I held in my hand and reached into my briefcase for a pen. When I found one, I turned the check over on my briefcase and endorsed it.

Looking up at Toni, sitting just a little over a foot away in the cramped lobby, I said, "I want you to have this," and handed her the check.

When she saw what it was, she shook her head vehemently. "No, I can't take that!"

"Please, I want you to have it. This isn't a decision I've just made. I've thought it over. It's for the baby."

Watching me with her mouth open, she looked flabbergasted.

"It's all I have to give you," I urged. "You'll need it. You'll have to buy baby clothes, baby furniture. And if you don't use it now, invest it for college." She looked at me as if I was speaking a language she couldn't comprehend. "It's the only way I have to say I'm truly sorry for everything I've done. Please, take it."

She searched my eyes, probably for any hidden agenda I might have. When she found none, only then did she reach out and take the check from my outstretched hand.

"Well, thank you, Beth. I honestly don't know what to say. I never expected—"

'You don't have to thank me," I said quickly. "Just take care of yourself and be happy." I stood and gathered up my briefcase. "If it's not too uncomfortable for you, keep in touch."

She rose from her seat. "I will."

We studied each other awkwardly for a moment, and then she gathered me into her arms and hugged me gently. I reluctantly pulled away and checked my watch.

"I have to get to work," I said. "I'll see you around." We said our good-byes, and I walked toward the elevator, surprising myself by not shedding a single tear until I was safely behind the closed steel doors.

Chapter Twenty-Five

The next days and week were a blur as I slowly recovered from the reopened wound of my break-up with Toni. It seemed every time I made it over one emotional hurdle, another one fell into my path, challenging me to keep trying to recover some semblance of a normal life. I wasn't sure I could ever be happy again, but I would have settled for just not being unhappy. I set my standards for happiness lower than they had been before I'd met Toni and plodded along, trying to stay busy enough to dull the pain to a bearable level.

After everything I had been hit with — seeing Toni with another woman, her planning a baby on her own, selling the house we lived in together, I knew it was time to move on with my life. Maybe in time, we could develop a friendship, but I had to admit, if only to myself, that I had demolished the relationship to the point that there was no chance of rebuilding it.

Laurel tried her best to keep me under her watchful eye. I knew she was worried about me, but she had no reason to be.

I frequently thought, with some bitterness, that I should have followed my instincts to decline when Laurel insisted I meet her friend in the first place. If I had kept my heart sheltered and continued with my one true love, my work, I would not be experiencing any of my current pain and heartbreak. I would have been content to continue swooning over Laurel and having one-night stands with random women who couldn't do damage to my heart.

I sat at my desk, looking out the window and pondering the mess my life had become. The seasons were changing again, and, just like all the other things in my life, I had no say in the matter. I just sat back and watched, a spectator who had no way to affect the outcome.

"Fuck it. Never again. No one is ever getting in here again." I pounded my chest with my palm, underscoring the promise I was making to myself, then folded my arms and leaned back in the office chair.

Kristy stepped into my office and took in my posture. "Taking a nap, or just plotting an overthrow of some sort?"

I turned my head toward her. "Neither. Just feeling sorry for myself."

She moved closer. "That's allowed every now and then. We're running out for some lunch. What can I get you?"

I shook my head as if the thought of eating disgusted me. Actually, it did.

"Beth, you have to eat something. You're wasting away."

She was right, but I didn't care. "I'm not hungry."

"All the more reason to eat something. It might boost your appetite. I'll be back with some soup." She was gone before I could argue.

I sat up and tried to shrug off my mood. I turned my

computer monitor on, and rubbed my eyes. I would eat whatever Kristy brought back for me, and would do my best to get out of the rut I was in, but I would never, ever permit myself fall in love again.

~ ~ ~

Two weeks later, I could see a change in myself. Work was becoming enjoyable again, and I immersed myself in project after project. The clients were pouring in, and I spent most of my waking hours staying on top of my accounts. At least those around me were not frequently wearing looks of worry on their faces.

Late on a Friday afternoon, I had just met with a new client, and I needed to run back to the office for some paperwork to take home with me for the weekend. I had bought a nearby condo with a bedroom large enough to house a small work area. That was where I spent most of my time when I was not in the studio.

I parked in my reserved spot behind the studio, where the gusting wind was creating paper and dust mini-tornadoes all around the parking lot. Squinting my eyes to shield them from the stinging dust, I ran to the back door.

Although everyone had left for the day, a dull light was glowing from the banker's lamp in my office. I knew Bryce had turned it on, knowing I'd be back in after my meeting. There were good people looking out for me, and the thought made me smile — the first genuine smile I'd had in a while.

I selected the files I needed from a filing cabinet, and went to turn off the lamp. I noticed the bright red glow on my phone. I had voicemail. I briefly considered whether to check the message or leave it for Monday. "Damn my work ethic anyway."

I dropped the files on the desk and punched in the code to listen to the message, checking my watch as the message began with a deep throat-clearing. There were some false starts on the caller's part before a voice, deep and clear and as familiar to me as my own, filled my office.

"Beth, uh, hi. Mmm, this is your da...your father. I'm calling because I wanted to let you know that your mom..." He stopped, and I could hear him gathering a deep breath. "Well, she passed away this afternoon. I know I have no right to ask you this, but if you could see your way clear to calling me..."

~ ~ ~

I had driven around the same block three times, trying to see the addresses that were obscured by the impending nightfall. I wasn't familiar with the neighborhood, but I knew what I was looking for. I decided to park my car in the first available spot and just hunt for the building on foot.

This area of town was beautiful, and I wondered for a second why Toni and I hadn't considered it when we were looking for a house. It seemed like that had been a million years ago, when I was someone else. So many thoughts raced through my head as I plodded down the even sidewalk. My mother had died. I had often wondered if I would be notified if anything happened to my parents. I had been sure I wouldn't. I didn't even know my father knew how to get in touch with me, but somehow he knew about my studio and how to reach me there.

I stopped in front of a small single-family home, modest, but clean and homey. I clutched the scrap of paper with the address on it and shone my phone on it to make sure I had the right address. Numb, I walked up to the door and rang the bell.

The door opened and Toni looked surprised, perhaps alarmed, to see me standing there.

"Beth!" Her mouth closed and opened, and her brow furrowed. She must have seen something in my face. "What's wrong?"

My face, so devoid of emotion until now, crumpled. I tried to hold back tears. "I didn't know where else to go."

Toni took my hand and gently pulled me inside and into an embrace. She had no idea why I was there, but knew that I needed the comfort of her arms. Despite everything I had put her through, she was willing to offer me comfort, and I drank it in.

"What happened? Tell me. Is Laurel okay?"

Unable to speak, I nodded. I sucked in a breath and swallowed. "My mom died." The tears came then, soundlessly.

Toni pulled me to her again and stroked my hair. "Oh, honey. Oh, I'm so sorry."

"I don't know how to feel, and you're the only one who understands. I didn't know where else to go."

"Shhhh. It's okay. You don't have to explain. I'm glad you're here." She slowly drew away from me and studied my face.

I tried to compose myself, embarrassed by my emotional outburst over a woman who hadn't cared a thing about me for at least fifteen years. "I don't know how to feel."

Toni cupped my cheek. "I know. I know, sweetie." She took my hand and led me into the living room, to the sofa, and had me sit. "I'll be right back. Don't go anywhere, okay?"

I nodded. Where would I go? Where could I go? I studied the room for the first time, memorizing each detail that reflected Toni's taste. I rubbed my hand along the sofa, covered in a sturdy, khaki-colored canvas. The windows were covered by interior wooden shutters, and a print area rug protected the hardwood floor. Toni's new house seemed like the perfect place to raise many happy children, I thought glumly.

Toni returned before my tears could begin again. She held a glass of water in one hand and a box of tissues in the other. She placed the water on the coffee table near my knee and handed me a tissue from the box before placing it next to the glass. She sat next to me, her hand resting on my knee.

"He called and left a message at the office."

If Toni didn't know who "he" was, she gave no indication.

I dabbed at my eyes with the tissue. "I called him back. I almost didn't. Didn't want to. I didn't want to hear that he's in pain over losing her. I didn't want him to ask me to be sorry that she's gone." More tears slipped out, and Toni rubbed my knee in silent comfort.

"Honey, it's okay to be angry. Don't beat yourself up."

"He wants me to go to the funeral."

Toni's hand stilled, and she tilted her head. I could tell she hadn't expected to hear that, any more than I'd expected to hear it from my father. Her brow creased, and her eyes narrowed.

"I think it's pretty selfish of your father to ask. What did you tell him?"

Underneath the pain I was feeling, a smile tried to form. Toni was angry with my father for asking something unspeakably painful of me. I knew I had run to the right person, despite the status of our relationship.

I rubbed my eyes, unmindful of the makeup I had applied earlier in the day. My eyes burned, and I wanted nothing more than to lie down and sleep.

Toni reached over and ran her thumb underneath my eye, her attempt to remove the smudge I'd undoubtedly made.

"I told him I would have to think about it. I told him I really didn't think that my mother would want me at her funeral, and he said he didn't care, because he wanted me there. I just don't know, Toni."

She wrapped me in her arms again. I reveled in the comfort her embrace provided.

"It's a lot to take in. You don't have to decide anything tonight. You'll have a clearer head about all of this tomorrow."

I reluctantly pulled away from her and grabbed a tissue from the box. I stood, eager to go home and crawl into bed. I swiped the tissue underneath both eyes and offered Toni a weak smile. "I guess I should go."

Toni stood and placed her hands on my shoulders. "You can stay as long as you'd like. Are you okay to drive?"

I nodded and pulled her into another hug. "Yeah, I'll be okay.

Thank you." As I held her, I could smell her shampoo. It flooded my mind with so many memories. I pushed away from her quickly and almost lost my balance.

"I'll give you a call tomorrow to see how you're doing, okay?" She tucked her hair behind her ear as she waited for my answer.

"I'll be okay, I promise. I'll let you know what I decide to do as far as the funeral goes."

"Good. Call me if you need me, or stop by if you need to talk. I... You know I'm always here for you, Beth, no matter what we've been through." She looked sad.

"Thanks again." I managed another weak smile and left the house, moving quickly to my car before I broke down and begged Toni to give us another try.

~ ~ ~

The morning of my mother's funeral, I went directly to the church. I knew my father wanted me to come to the funeral home beforehand, but I needed to draw some line in the sand. If I'm being kind, the only thing I can say about my mother is that she barely tolerated me for much of my adult life. I wasn't about to give her even a morsel of respect now, and I was feeling only slightly more tolerant of my father, because he had taken the first step and called me.

The cloying scent of flowers hung in the air, and the organ music resounded in my head. I was sitting alone, near the back, not yet ready for my father to see me. I watched him follow the casket into the church.

Fidgeting and straightening my dress, I looked around and wondered what I was doing there. I was eager to leave. A panic attack seemed imminent.

I was beginning to regret turning down Laurel's offer to come with me. I told her it was something I had to do alone, and that I didn't plan on being gone long. I figured it would take five hours, more or less — the drive up here and back, the service, and a quick chat with my father, which might or might not happen. There was no reason for Laurel to miss a day of work over my mother. It was unsettling enough that I had decided to.

The mourners rose and sat, and rose and knelt, and I mindlessly followed along, each second wishing that I hadn't come. I didn't belong there. I didn't know anyone among the grieving. As for the few blood relatives in attendance —I barely knew them. The graveside ceremony would be for family only, but I wasn't going to the cemetery. I no longer considered myself in the "family" category.

The church service ended, and I hung back in the line of people waiting to give my father their condolences. I watched him as he stood near the hearse, greeting those who wanted to hug him, shake his hand, or give him a consoling clap on the back.

When he saw me, we both froze. My father shook a few more hands and then excused himself. Time crawled as he walked toward me, a sad, tentative smile on his face. Despite the years that had passed since I last saw him, I was surprised by how old he looked.

"Beth."

There was gratitude in his voice, and I didn't know how to react to it.

He reached out as if to hug me, then thought better of it. Instead he placed his hands on my shoulders and squeezed.

"Hi, Dad." My throat tightened, and my voice squeaked. I could sense others were watching us.

"I'm so glad you could make it, sweetheart. Will you come to the cemetery?"

My stomach roiled. I was determined to avoid that. "I don't think so, Dad. I really need to get back home."

He tried to hide his disappointment. "You've grown into a beautiful woman. I hear you're doing really well for yourself, too." He looked away, took a deep breath, then looked back at me.

"Could I maybe call you in a few days, so we can talk? Would that be okay?"

There were many things I wanted to say to him, but this wasn't the time. He looked so unsure of himself, it broke my heart. Even though my father had turned his back on me, either willingly or under pressure from my mother, I found it hard to turn my back on him completely.

"Sure, Dad." I hugged him. "I really have to go now."

He gave me a slight wave before turning back toward the hearse.

I brushed a few tears from my eyes as I went to my car. I gazed up at the brilliant sky and hoped it might be a sign of better things to come.

~ ~ ~

I sat at the polished wooden table in the studio's conference room, trying my best to keep my focus on the client who was sitting across from me, stroking his goatee.

Bryce was manning the data projector, which splashed potential branding materials for the client's business onto the screen at the end of the narrow room.

The room was sealed tighter than a sarcophagus, and hot sweat trickled down between my shoulder blades. I was grateful that Bryce was handling the presentation, because all I could think of was getting out of the room before a panic attack struck. They'd been coming with more frequency.

"Well, I like the designs very much, so let's get started on the whole package. Letterhead, logo, website, everything." The client looked at me with toothy grin.

I returned the smile, hoping I didn't look as if I was cringing. *Hold on just a few more minutes, and you'll be out of here.* I discreetly mopped my brow as I stood and extended my hand toward the door, hoping the client would take the hint and move in that direction. He did.

I followed him through the door, assuring him I would keep him abreast of the progress on his campaign. I kept my eye on my steps, controlling my breath and telling myself over and over that I could make it. Halfway through the main studio area, I looked up.

Toni was sitting in the waiting area. Her mouth turned up

in the smallest of smiles when our eyes met.

I stumbled as my left foot kicked the heel of my right foot, and the client reached out and grasped my elbow.

"Everything okay?" he asked.

I smiled another phony smile. *I'm getting pretty good at this.* "I'm fine, thank you. As I was saying, you should be hearing from me early next week, and I'll let you know how close we are to being finished." I shook his hand and held the door open to facilitate his exit.

Taking a deep breath and releasing it slowly, I turned around. I closed my eyes for a second, and when I opened them, Toni was still there, so I crossed over to where she was sitting on a small sofa, hands clasped.

My brain scrambled to match Toni with this setting. My mouth formed an "O", but I made no sound.

Toni stood. "Hi, Beth. I'm really sorry I just dropped in like this. I hope you don't mind."

I shook my head as I bit the inside of my cheek. I could feel the anxiety attack slowly ebbing away, and I breathed a sigh of relief. "No, I don't mind. Is everything okay?"

"Yes, yeah, I'm fine. I just…" She looked across the studio at my employees, who were trying to appear as if they were working instead of hanging on our every word. "Could we maybe talk in your office?"

I glanced down and noticed the beginnings of a baby bump. With a nod, I spun on my heel, careful not to trip again, and headed toward my office. I could hear the click clack of her shoes close behind me. *Dear Lord, I don't know what she wants, but please help me.* I stood at the door and let her enter my office before I followed her inside and shut the door behind me. Feeling as if I was running on auto-pilot, I extended my arm toward the sofa, much as I had done to hurry my client along just minutes before.

Toni sat down and faced me, then waited for me to take my seat. "How are you, Beth?"

I rubbed my neck and looked around the room. "Um, well, you know…"

Silence filled the room as Toni waited for me to finish the sentence. When I didn't speak, she said, "You've lost weight."

I looked down at my dress, which hung on me. "Yeah, a little. I forget to eat sometimes." My eyes moved everywhere but to her.

"We haven't spoken since the night your mother died, and I really needed to see how you are."

"Oh." I finally looked at her. I hadn't returned her calls or updated her since that night at her house. Things just felt too complicated.

Her eyes held nothing but compassion.

I folded my arms around my midsection and sat back in the sofa, turning toward her. "Thank you. It's been a weird couple of weeks, to say the least." I flashed another phony smile.

"Do you want to talk about it?"

"Mmm, well. Not much to say, really." I tucked a loose strand of hair behind my ear. This was feeling very surreal.

"So, you went."

"Yeah, I went. Didn't have much of a chance to talk to my dad, but he sent me a long letter afterwards. Pretty much blamed everything on my mother." I grew quiet again.

"Beth."

I looked over at Toni. There was concern on her face.

"Things have actually been," I rolled my eyes toward the ceiling, looking for the right descriptive, "weird, but okay. After his letter, my dad and I started talking. He calls me once a week, and we just talk about...things." I looked at her. "Sometimes he cries. He feels so bad about how he treated me and all." I wasn't sure what else to say. "I guess it's going to take some time."

Toni placed her hand on my forearm. "Of course it's going to take some time! Your parents disowned you and haven't talked to you for how long now? Fifteen years?"

I nodded. I rubbed the scar on my forehead and looked away again.

"This is a lot to deal with, especially after... Well, you know. I'm concerned about you, Beth. You really are too thin."

I faced her again. Her eyes were beginning to swim. *Oh, please, don't start crying. If you do, I'll cry too, and I might never stop.*

She tilted her head and waited patiently for me to say something.

I nodded acknowledgement of her worry. "I promise you, I'm fine. At least I'm on the road back to being fine. This is just another bump in the road, and it's not necessarily a bad one. I never would have guessed that my dad and I would be talking again."

She smiled and rested her hand on mine. "Promise me you'll start eating better."

"Okay."

"Can I ask for one more thing?"

I managed a small smile. "Sure, why not?"

She took a deep breath and watched me closely. "Do you think that we could maybe work on getting our friendship back?"

The silence of the room pounded in my head and made me wonder if I had heard her correctly. She bit her lip. That had always been her nervous gesture.

"Yes, yeah, okay, I guess. Are you... Is that what you want? Are you ready for that?"

She grinned and pushed away some hair that had fallen across her face. She tucked it behind her ear. "Yeah, I would like that a lot. I...I'd like to see if we can salvage that."

"I'd like that too," I murmured.

She beamed as she stood. "Okay, then. I'm going to call you soon to see how you're doing, and maybe we can have lunch or something?" She looked confident, but her voice betrayed her.

It struck me that she was as scared as I was.

I rose from the sofa and stood next to her, confused by my mixed feelings.

Her smile disappeared and serious Toni took over. "If you need to talk to someone about this stuff with your dad," she motioned her hands back and forth in front of her, "I'm here. I know you have Laurel, but if you need me…"

I nodded.

"Call me soon. Promise me."

"I promise."

"Okay, good, we'll talk soon."

She gathered me into an embrace, and I melted. Recognizing its home, my body folded into hers. I sighed into her hair; it still smelled as I remembered. I was in danger of crying, so I pulled away from her quickly. "I'll walk you out," I offered.

"No, I'm fine. Stay and get your work done. I know how busy you are." She smiled again, studied my face for another instant, and then headed toward the door with a wave to my staff as I watched from my office door.

I shrugged and headed toward the small kitchen in the back of the studio. "I guess I'd better get something to eat so I can keep my promise." I heard Bryce's whisper when he thought I was far enough away that I wouldn't hear.

"Hallelujah."

Chapter Twenty-Six

As she had suggested, Toni and I had lunch, and over the following months, we saw each other regularly. We still weren't comfortable enough with each other to build an easy friendship, but we were trying. One evening at the beginning of summer, I pulled into Laurel and Will's driveway after an excruciatingly long day at the studio, wanting nothing more than to convince Laurel to see a movie with me.

The sound of music blaring from a radio was coming from the back of the house, and I walked around and found Laurel's oldest lying on a towel in the backyard, attempting to bake herself to a golden hue.

"Hey, Kira, how's it going?"

She barely lifted her head, grunted, and informed me in as few words as possible that her mother was in the kitchen. She gestured vaguely in that general direction. I shrugged as I recalled how, only a few weeks before, I had laughed as I teased Laurel about having to deal with a pre-pubescent and her mood swings. It appeared that I would also be favored with her attitude.

Shaking my head, I went in the back door and bounded into the kitchen, where I found Laurel chatting with Toni. There was always the chance that I would find her there, since she had moved within walking distance.

"Hi," they chorused in unison.

Toni was leaning against the counter, eating slices of apple. I noticed that her belly jutted out even more than it had the previous time I'd seen her.

I dropped into one chair, propped my feet up on another, and waited for a lull in their conversation. They were talking about school and people I didn't know, so I tried to relax and forget about my hectic day until they stopped speaking. When they looked at me at, I took it as a sign to jump in before they started up again.

"Let's order some dinner and then go out to a movie," I said, including them both in my invitation.

"Sounds good to me," Laurel answered, and turned to Toni.

"I can't," she replied, popping the last of the apple into her mouth. "I'm going out with Susan Winters tonight."

Even after all the time we'd been apart, my stomach churned at the thought of Toni going out with another woman. Laurel had informed me that Leah was history, but she insisted she didn't know if Toni was seeing anyone else.

Laurel caught my reaction and turned back to Toni, her brow furrowing. "I didn't know Susan was gay," she blurted.

Holding her stomach, Toni laughed loudly. "She's not! We're just friends."

Though her laughter stopped, her hand remained on her stomach, which Laurel noted.

"What's wrong? Are you all right?" she asked.

Toni nodded and smiled. "Baby's kicking."

Laurel squealed and rushed to place her hand next to Toni's, then she stood still, barely breathing. After a second, they both laughed, and Laurel removed her hand. I remained seated, uncomfortably watching their exchange.

Toni came over to me. "Would you like to feel the baby kick?" she asked with a grin.

Speechless at first, I finally managed to mutter, "Okay."

Toni took my hand in hers and placed it where she'd felt the last kick. It took a few moments for the baby to move forcefully enough for me to feel, but when it happened at last, the sensation was amazing. I felt the pushing beneath my palm, and Toni's warm hand pressed mine against her stomach. "Thank you," I said with a smile.

"I'd better run, or I'll be late." Toni gathered her things and went to the door. "Enjoy your night out."

Then she was gone, leaving me feeling happier than I had in months.

Chapter Twenty-Seven

I parked my Jag in my designated space behind the studio and was about to lock the car, when I saw Toni walking toward me. Intrigued, I closed the door and met her halfway.

"What's wrong?" I asked, immediately concerned as to why she would be coming to see me at work.

"Nothing. I was driving by and saw you pull in, so I thought that I'd stop and say 'hi.' Is that all right?"

I was relieved but perplexed. "Sure. Come on in, and we can have coffee."

We walked into the studio side by side, and found Bryce humming to himself as he brewed coffee, his usual morning routine. He smiled when he saw me, and his eyebrows rose when he saw Toni.

She greeted him warmly. "Hi, Bryce. How are things?"

"Toni, it's been so long!" He hurried across the room and gathered her into his arms. "How are you?"

I left them to their catching up while I went into my office and organized some of the work on my desk. After a moment, Toni came in and closed the door behind her. She was grinning as she moved closer to me.

"Sit down," I offered. "Tell me what's going on."

"Nothing earth shattering, so calm down. I can see the worry written all over your face."

She still knew me, I thought, as I perched on the corner of the desk.

"I just wanted to tell you that I'm glad we've been so successful at rebuilding our friendship. I've missed you." She sat down in one of the office chairs and gazed up at me hopefully, biting her bottom lip ever so slightly.

A smile began slowly, then widened on my face. "That means a lot to me." I beamed, mirroring her smile. We chatted awhile longer. It seemed to me that Toni had dropped in mainly to make sure I was all right, and I was fine with that. It warmed me to know that she cared enough to go out of her way to check on me.

She rose and hugged me gently. "I have to get going, but maybe we can have lunch again soon?"

"Sure."

I floated out of the office as I escorted her out, ecstatic to have her back in my life in even the slightest way. We stopped at her car, and she paused before getting inside. She squeezed my hand, climbed into the car, and pulled away.

Humming, I checked my watch as I walked back inside. The entire incident had taken no more than ten minutes, but the feeling it left me with would last for days.

Bryce watched me expectantly as I ambled toward him, almost drunk with giddiness.

"I know you want to know what that was about," I teased.

"Go ahead and ask."

"Well?"

"Toni came by to say that she's thankful for having me back in her life. It seems that she feels we've finally reached a place where we can be friends."

"That's great. But does that mean that you might be able to work things out with her?" he wondered aloud.

I frowned as I mulled over his question. The thought hadn't even crossed my mind. I was at first relieved that she wasn't here to bring me bad news, and then elated when I found out what the news was.

"It didn't come up, and it didn't really cross my mind. Honestly, as much as I would love for a reconciliation between us, I wouldn't hold my breath. I don't think it's likely to happen."

Bryce was pondering that when suddenly his face brightened. "I didn't know she was so far along! When is she due?"

I was embarrassed to say, "I'm not sure, but it sure looked like it could be any day."

I strode back into my office, ready to start the day with an uplifting new outlook.

Chapter Twenty-Eight

My first thought when I awoke was that there was a teapot whistling in my apartment. I pulled the covers over my head and rolled over, wishing someone would come and take the kettle off the stove. The sound persisted, waking me completely, and I realized that it was the phone ringing. I stumbled from the bed and out to the kitchen, where the phone sat on the counter.

"Hello," I muttered, glancing at the clock on the stove and seeing that I would have had to get up for work in another half hour anyway.

"Beth, it's me," Laurel replied breathlessly.

"I should have known. Only you would get me out of bed this early. You have a sadistic streak, you know that?" I rubbed the sleep from my eyes and yawned noisily.

"I wanted to be the first to tell you the news, but if that's your attitude, maybe I shouldn't tell you at all."

I could tell that she was smiling, so I decided to play along. "Great! I can still get another half hour of sleep in. Talk to you later."

"Toni's had her baby!" she squealed. "It's a girl. They're both doing fine."

I was utterly speechless as conflicting emotions swept through me. I was happy for Toni. I knew she wanted this child with her whole being. More than she wanted me, apparently, I thought with a tinge of leftover self-pity. A tiny bit of sadness stemmed from the fact that I still loved Toni, and I should have been with her during all this.

"Is Toni okay? How is she? What's the baby's name? Has she told you?"

"She's fine, just very tired. It was a long labor. She apparently already knew it would be a girl. She's had the name ready for months." Laurel paused dramatically. "She named her Anabeth." She finished with a chuckle, knowing how that news would affect me.

Surprised, I nevertheless smiled as I pulled a kitchen chair closer and lowered myself into it. Anabeth was my given name. Toni had always loved it, and had often scolded me for going by the shortened version, Beth. "Why did she do that?" I asked Laurel.

"I don't know, and I didn't ask."

"What should I do? Should I go to the hospital?" I wasn't sure what the role of an ex was in this situation.

"I would wait. She's sleeping a lot right now. She'll be going home tomorrow, you can see her there. You might want to give her some time to rest, and then call her later on today," Laurel suggested.

I hung up and went to take a hot shower to clear my head. Despite the good news, and the fact that Toni's life had changed completely, I knew that it was still just another day at the office for me as I hurried to get to the studio.

~ ~ ~

The following evening I was on Toni's doorstep, anxiously waiting for an answer to my knock. I had called her earlier, and she agreed enthusiastically when I asked if I could come see her and the baby.

The door was opened by Grace, Toni's mother, and I tensed in anticipation of how she might act at seeing me for the first time since my break-up with her daughter.

She greeted me with a broad smile that was so like her daughter's. "Beth! It's so good to see you!"

Warmed by her greeting and obvious lack of animosity, I immediately relaxed. I followed her into the living room, where Toni was holding a small blanketed bundle. The sunlight through the window behind her framed her hair and darkened her face, but I could see her radiant smile.

"I'll be in the kitchen if you need me," Grace said to her daughter. She squeezed my hand and left us alone in the room.

"Have a seat," Toni said, the smile apparently permanently affixed to her face.

I lowered myself onto the sofa. "How do you feel?"

"I feel wonderful. I'm still tired, but Mom's helping out with the baby, and that lets me get some rest." She sat beside me and tilted Anabeth toward me so that I could see her face. "Well, here she is."

Her unbelievably tiny daughter was sleeping soundlessly.

The thin blanket was draped up over the top of her head, but I could see small wisps of black hair peeking out from underneath. She had a pug nose and puckered lips, and her closed eyes were framed with long black lashes. I couldn't tear my eyes from her.

"Would you like to hold her?" she asked softly.

"Can I?"

"Of course." She handed the baby to me, and I held her carefully, remembering to support her tiny head and neck. I took one of her little hands in my own, fascinated at the difference in size.

"You're the first one to see her," Toni said.

I felt a rush of pride. "Really?"

"Yes. Except for Mom, of course. She's been here for over a week, but Dad won't be coming until the weekend."

"She looks just like you," I murmured in amazement.

Toni laughed. "It's too early to see a resemblance." Her fingers trailed lightly through her daughter's feathery curls.

"No, I see it," I argued. "Her coloring is the same as yours." She tilted her head, as if assessing the truth of my observation. "I remember your baby pictures, Toni. You looked just like this."

She leaned back on the sofa with a grin. "You sound like Mom."

"You look great." I tried not to gush, but didn't know what else to say.

"Thanks. You do too."

"I have a gift in the car. I didn't want to bring it in with me because it's kind of big. I didn't want to overwhelm you." I laughed at the thought of the enormous stuffed bear that was taking up most of my back seat.

"My God, Beth, it was more than enough that you gave Anabeth your share of the sale of the house. You didn't have to bring anything."

"I wanted to. When I saw it in a store, I knew it was something no newborn should have to do without."

Toni sighed, resigning herself to accepting another gift. "Well, thank you. Why don't you give her to me? I'll put her to bed."

I handed the baby back with a bit of regret. When Toni came back, I didn't know how to express how much seeing Anabeth had touched me, so instead I just said, "She's a beautiful baby, Toni."

She sat next to me on the sofa and turned toward me. "Thank you for coming, Beth. I wasn't sure if you'd want to see her."

"Of course I did. Toni, I know that my reaction to you wanting to have a baby wasn't what you anticipated, but I hope you know that nothing that happened between us would ever affect how I treat her."

Toni nodded. "I know that. I just didn't know if you it would be too painful for you to see Anabeth."

I beamed. "Anabeth."

"Yes." My smile was returned.

"Why?"

Toni took a long moment to find the words to answer. "Well, for one thing, you have a beautiful name. I've told you countless times how much I love it. But the main reason is that you're a special person in my life. You always will be. We've had some difficult times over the last year and a half, but I've always loved you."

At my shocked expression, she said, "I know I haven't always treated you in a loving way. Actually, I've been pretty cruel to you at times. Let me finish," she said when she saw me shaking my head.

"I've wanted to say something for a while now, but couldn't find a way to begin. What I'm trying to explain is that you've touched my life in a way that no one ever has, and even though we're not together anymore, I want you to always be in my life. That includes Anabeth now, too. I want her to grow up knowing you, and I thought that one way to ensure that happens would be to tie her to you with your name. Even if you want no part of her, at least she'll have that."

Tears were spilling over Toni's cheeks, and they began to well in my own eyes. I took both of her hands and held them tightly.

"Of course I want to be a part of her life. It's more than I could have hoped for, considering I destroyed our relationship by convincing myself I didn't want a baby."

She pulled me into her arms, and we cried together. When I pulled away, I knew I had to finish saying what I had been trying to tell her for months.

"I know what happened between us. I've thought it all out, and I know that I acted the way I did because I was scared. In the back of my mind, I saw my parents and how they raised me." I wiped my tears with the back of my hand, and my explanation spilled out in a rush of words as Toni listened to it for the first time.

"When I was growing up, they were strict, but at least they gave me love, their version of it, anyway. Despite that, they disowned me when they found out I'm gay.

"When you were talking about having a baby, it terrified me to think that I would be responsible for another person, for loving that child, and I began to worry. What if my love wasn't enough, just like my parents' love wasn't strong enough to keep loving me no matter what? What if our child grew into someone I didn't approve of? Would I be like my parents and turn my back?

"My God, Toni. The thought frightened and sickened me! I couldn't have lived with myself if I inflicted as much pain on our child as my parents did to me."

Tears streamed down my face, and Toni pulled me into her embrace.

"I pushed you away so I wouldn't have to deal with that possibility, but I went too far." My voice hitching with tears, I barely managed to whisper, "I never meant to lose you."

"Shhhh. Don't cry." Toni stroked my hair and held me until my tears stopped, then she handed me a tissue.

"I didn't mean to upset you," she apologized as I wiped my nose. "It's good that we talked, though. It's been a long time coming." When I nodded, she smiled. "Why don't we go out to your car and get Anabeth's gift."

We were quiet as we walked outside, until Toni spied the bear in the back seat. "Oh, it's adorable! I had no idea they made stuffed animals that big."

I hoisted it from the seat and followed Toni back into the house.

Toni popped her head into the kitchen. "Mom, come see what Beth brought."

The three of us talked a while longer, but when I noticed how tired Toni was, I knew it was time for me to leave. "I guess I better go and let you get some rest while Anabeth is asleep." Grace gave me a hug, and Toni walked me out.

"I'm glad you came over."

"So am I." I gave her a hug.

"Come over again soon. We can go out to lunch or something."

"I'll give you a call so we can set something up." Whistling happily, I got into my car and headed home.

Chapter Twenty-Nine

Before I knew it, another Christmas was upon me. It was my second holiday season without Toni. Having her back in my life platonically didn't fill the void in my life that had been there since our separation. I was still lonely, though I was definitely handling my time alone better than I had the previous Christmas.

Toni was taking Anabeth to Delaware to spend the baby's first Christmas with her family. I was invited to spend the holiday with Laurel and Will, but I was hoping that Toni would return before New Year's Eve, and that we could spend that evening together.

My father had asked me to spend the holiday with him, but it felt like too much, too soon. I decided instead to spend Christmas day with Laurel, Will, and the girls.

Gifts in tow, I let myself into Will and Laurel's house mid-afternoon on Christmas Day. The frigid air had chilled me on the short walk from the car to the house, so I set the packages under the tree, removed my gloves and warmed myself by the fireplace before I went to find my friends.

I heard music coming from one of the upstairs bedrooms, and assumed that Kira or Becca was enjoying a new gift. I followed the clattering sounds coming from the kitchen. The warm room was rich with the smell of cooking food, and Laurel, Kira, and Will were preparing dinner.

"Ho, ho, ho," I greeted, arms outstretched. I hugged each of them and offered to help with dinner.

"Nope," Laurel replied. "You're our guest today. No helping out for you. Besides, everything is just about ready, so plant yourself in the dining room and we'll be with you shortly. Kira, please go get your sister."

Laurel set about transferring dinner into bowls and onto platters. I stood watching until she looked up.

"All right, Beth. If you really want to do something, you can get the drinks ready," she said.

I went into the dining room and poured wine for the three of us and warm cider, which Will had prepared for the girls. Feeling I had earned my keep, I sat down and waited for my surrogate family to join me. First, Becca and Kira bounded down the stairs, and Becca hugged me before the two went into the kitchen to help. Within minutes, all four came in carrying the Christmas feast to the table.

During dinner, we talked about everything from how the girls were doing in school, to plans for New Year's Eve. Kira and Becca participated in the conversation, and I was struck by how grown up the girls were, and how proud I was of how Will and Laurel were raising them. They were so well-adjusted, so mature, they seemed older than they actually were. Laurel beamed at her daughters, appearing relieved that Kira's teenager attitude had been put on hold for the day.

"You have all made this a wonderful day for me." I looked at each of them. "Thank you."

"It would have been more interesting if Mom would have invited that woman she wants you to meet," Becca piped up.

Laurel made one of the most mortified faces I'd ever seen on her, and Kira kicked her sister under the table.

"Ow! What?" Becca whined.

"What woman, Becca?" I was afraid I already knew the answer.

My question was met by guilty silence, and no one met my gaze. Even Will focused on shoveling food into his mouth.

"Tell me what's going on," I demanded.

With a sigh, Kira confessed, "Mom thinks it's time you get a new girlfriend, and she was gonna invite someone she knows to have dinner with us today."

I was dismayed. "Oh, God. Not this again. Laurel, just how many lesbians do you know?"

"It turned out that she's with someone," Laurel began, "but you do need to find someone. You know we worry about you."

I stared at her for some time before breaking into laughter. My attack of the giggles belied the anger I was attempting to convey. "I should disown you," I said half-heartedly. "Please don't try to set me up with anyone right now. I'm just getting my life back on track."

"Okay, no more matchmaking." Laurel smiled impishly. "At least for now."

"I don't get why you and Aunt Toni hang out all the time," Kira commented. "It's just weird."

"Yeah." Becca put in her two cents worth. "My friend's mom and dad got divorced, and they hate each other."

I saw the amused expression on Laurel's face challenging me to explain.

"Well, Toni and I had a very solid relationship," I began, trying to figure it out myself as I went along. "Sometimes when a relationship is that good, it's strong enough to sustain a friendship after a break-up." I was pleased with myself for coming up with such a believable explanation.

"If you had such a great relationship, why'd you break up?"

Kira's question held no animosity. It was fueled by a fifteen-year-old's curiosity. I knew her parents had not gone into detail about our separation, feeling the girls were both too young to understand at the time. I found the subject difficult to discuss, even after all the time that had passed, but it was an honest question that deserved a response.

"Toni and I broke up because we both made some mistakes and it was impossible to stay together because of the pain we caused each other. Also, Toni wanted a baby, and I wasn't sure that having a baby was something I wanted. It's very difficult to maintain a relationship when the people involved want opposite things. One of us would have had to make an enormous sacrifice."

A frown crinkling her nose, Becca looked at me across the table. "I thought you cheated on Aunt Toni."

"Becca!" Will scolded.

"Where did you hear that?" Laurel seemed sure that she and Will had been careful when discussing the matter with one another.

"I don't know." Becca shrugged. "I guess I just thought that from hearing you guys talk." I smiled at Becca so she wouldn't feel so bad about her bluntness. "Let's just say that I made more mistakes than Toni did, but we've managed to forgive each other enough to be friends. And that's not weird," I added with a smile.

After the table had been cleared and gifts had been opened, the girls retired to their rooms, and Laurel, Will, and I moved to the living room with a pot of coffee.

"I'm sorry about the grilling," Will said with a sheepish grin.

"I had no idea they knew so many of the details. They must have read between the lines and come up with their own conclusions," Laurel added, shaking her head.

"That's all right. I don't mind answering their questions. You should be pleased that they're so conscious of what goes on around them." I sipped my coffee. "And they sure don't settle for pat answers. Wonder where they get that from." I shot a pointed look at Laurel.

We all laughed and settled in to watch *It's a Wonderful Life*.

Chapter Thirty

The next several months, Toni and I spent much of our spare time together. Sometimes we would stay with the baby; other times, Laurel would babysit and we'd go out alone.

All the time we spent together was not lost on our friends. One day, at the office, Bryce nonchalantly asked, "Have you and Toni reconciled?

I laughed. "Are you kidding me? I thought we went through this months ago. The answer is still the same."

I didn't give it another thought until a few weeks later, on a chilly midwinter day, when Laurel posed a similar query.

We were sitting together on the floor of her living room, enjoying a rare moment alone. Will had shepherded the girls, along with some of their friends, to the mall. Laurel had invited both me and Toni to dinner, and we had at least half an hour before she was due to arrive. My legs were stretched out in front of me, my back resting against the front of the sofa. Laurel sat across from me, her legs also stretched out in front of her, as we both sipped hot, lemony tea.

We were discussing Kira's rebellious attitude, and the subject somehow turned to Anabeth. At the mention of the baby's name, my face lit up.

Laurel smiled tenderly. "You love her like she's your own, don't you?"

"Yeah, I do," I said without hesitation. "I look at her, and I wonder what I was so afraid of."

Suddenly Laurel blurted, "Beth, if you and Toni were back together, you would have told me, wouldn't you?"

I nearly spilled my tea. "Where did that come from?"

"You two aren't back together, are you?"

I raised my eyebrow and I set my cup on the coffee table. "No, we're not. Whatever gave you that crazy idea?"

"Do you realize how much time you two spend together?" When I didn't reply, she answered her own question, ticking off each bit of evidence on her fingers. "You go out to dinner at least once a week. You see each other a few times in between. God only knows how many phone conversations you have, and, I'm not complaining, but I watch Anabeth once or twice a month so you two can go out alone. Beth, for all intents and purposes, you two are dating!"

I opened my mouth, but she continued before I could utter a syllable.

"And then there's how you look at each other."

My brow furrowed in confusion, and then I realized how our friendship could appear from the outside. "Wait a minute. I can maybe, and that's a big maybe, see how you might misinterpret the amount of time Toni and I spend together, but you lost me with that last one. Exactly how do we look at each other?"

Laurel smiled at knowing she had pushed a button in me somewhere. "You look at each other the way you used to. Maybe not directly at each other, but when Toni's talking to someone else, you look at her with love in your eyes."

I could feel a warm blush creeping up my neck to my face. I had thought that I was successfully keeping my emotions veiled, trying to content myself with at least having a friendship with Toni.

"Well, I...I..." I stared at my hands, averting my eyes from the look of pity I was sure I'd see on Laurel's face. "You know I'll always love Toni. I didn't mean for it to be obvious."

"Beth, wake up! Toni looks at you the same way."

"She what?" I knew how goofy I must look with my mouth hanging open in surprise, but I was gobsmacked.

"She does, Beth. Why do you think I thought you were back together?"

"I...I think you're imagining things, Laurel. She's given no indication that she wants anything more than the friendship we have now."

"Don't get testy with me! I'm just making an observation."

Laurel smiled at my discomfort, confirming the known fact that she was the most masochistic friend I've ever had.

She kicked my foot, which rested just inches from hers. "You know I love you like a sister, and nothing would make me happier than seeing you and Toni work things out and get back together. But even if you don't, that's okay, because at least the old you is back."

She gathered me into a hug, and that was how Toni found us when walked into the house, carrying Anabeth.

She stopped short. "Am I interrupting something?" she

asked, only half kidding.

"Nope," Laurel answered. "Just bonding."

But for the first time in almost two years, I began thinking that there might yet be some hope for Toni and me.

Chapter Thirty-One

I was at my desk shuffling through the month's invoices when Bryce sauntered into the room.

"Hey, boss, what do you have scheduled for tonight?"

I set the invoices aside and pretended to check my calendar. "Hmm...the same as last Friday, as well as next Friday. Nothing."

"Great! There's a wonderful new club opening, and I don't want to go alone."

"Gosh, Bryce, I'm glad you don't go for the mushy approach, such as 'I'd like to spend some time with you.' You go right to the 'I'm lonely' guilt trip approach," I teased.

"Come on, you know what I meant. Call Toni, and we'll make a night of it."

I pretended that I was mulling the offer, but the truth was that once Bryce mentioned including Toni, the invitation became much more appealing.

"I'll see what she says." I lifted the receiver and punched in Toni's cell phone number.

Toni's only reservation at joining us was that she felt she was relying too much on Laurel as a babysitter. I knew Laurel didn't mind , and offered to contact her myself. As I knew she would, Laurel readily agreed to watch Anabeth.

Later that evening, the three of us were on the second floor of the crowded three-story club. There was a large bar, tables, and a jukebox. Upstairs was a dance floor, and downstairs was a game room, complete with pool tables and video games.

"Let's grab some drinks and go down to the pool tables," Bryce suggested. He took our drink orders and went off to the bar. When he returned, he had three glasses precariously in hand.

"Let's go," he directed, preceding us to the stairs.

Bryce was racking the balls while we sorted out who would play whom first, when we were approached by a tall blonde with blazing blue eyes.

"Do you guys need a fourth?" she asked me directly.

When I didn't answer promptly, Bryce answered. "We sure do."

The blonde introduced herself as Megan, and after we reciprocated, she asked me if Toni and I were together.

"No, we're not," Toni answered, a little too quickly. "We're just friends."

She gave me a little push in Megan's direction. I turned to Bryce, who was watching with more than a little amusement. I glared at him for his lack of assistance.

We paired off, and during the first two games we played, it was apparent that Megan was interested in getting to know me better. I was not only uncomfortable, I was not interested.

After the second game, Megan said, "Winner buys a round."

She had barely walked away from our table before I cornered

Bryce, who was giggling at my embarrassment.

"Shouldn't you be out looking for your new flavor of the month?" I asked with more cattiness than Bryce deserved. He held his own, though.

"Well, honey, it beats being celibate for the last...what is it, almost two years now?"

I thanked any higher power there might be for the darkened room as I felt my face flush. I glanced at Toni and found her watching me. I found it hard to read the look on her face.

"Megan likes you," Bryce said.

I tore my eyes from Toni's and looked at Bryce, then turned back to Toni as she said quietly, "Bryce's right, she does like you. If I'm making you uncomfortable, I can leave." She didn't sound angry.

"No! I have no interest in her, or anyone for that matter." I turned toward Bryce. "And if I'm celibate, it's at least by choice, so I'm counting on you, Mr. Matchmaker, to keep her away from me."

They both laughed then, and agreed to help me deflect any advances from Megan, who was returning with our drinks. Though Bryce and Toni both did their best to help me dissuade her, I left the club that evening with Megan's phone number.

~ ~ ~

It was weeks later, early March, and I was standing in front of my open office window, enjoying the warmth that promised spring would soon be returning. I was thinking about the happenings of the past couple of months, wondering where Toni and I were headed.

She hadn't brought up the incident at the nightclub, and I wasn't sure what her take on it had been. She had seemed surprised when Bryce said that I hadn't been with anyone since our break-up, but she hadn't said anything to me, and I certainly wasn't about to broach the subject myself.

As I thought back to that evening, it seemed to me as if she had looked resigned when she'd offered to leave. It was almost as if she had just realized that I might want a relationship with someone else, and she thought she might be keeping me from it.

I looked down at the invitation I was holding. It was for the showing of a local artist at an exclusive gallery in town. Normally, I would have declined, but the display was also an AIDS benefit, and when I'd mentioned it to Toni, she had shown some interest in attending, so I'd accepted.

I sighed and folded the invitation. I had to have a talk with Toni.

Chapter Thirty-Two

The evening at the art gallery was the beginning of the end as far as denying my feelings for Toni was concerned. I arrived at the gallery a short time before our planned meeting time. I helped myself to some wine from a tray being carried by a passing waiter, and casually inspected the art on display.

After a cursory glance at the artist's work, I worked my way back toward the reception area. I was pleased to see that Toni had just arrived, and that she had Anabeth in tow.

"Hi." I reached for Anabeth so that Toni could remove her coat. "Hello, sweetie," I cooed to the smiling girl in my arms, amazed at how quickly she was growing.

My attention quickly switched from Anabeth to her mother. The basic black dress Toni was wearing beneath her coat reminded me of the first time we'd met.

"You look stunning," I said with what little breath was left in my lungs. She'd always looked this beautiful, I reminded myself, but there was something about her tonight.

"Thank you. You look pretty great yourself," she said, giving me the once-over.

"This place looks dead. Maybe we could keep it short and run out for a bite to eat?" I suggested hopefully.

"Sure. I want to see the pieces, but I wasn't planning on staying late anyway," she answered, leaving the ball in my court.

I hoisted the baby onto my hip and handed Toni the drink I'd been holding. "Hold this, and I'll get one for you."

I took Anabeth with me to the open bar, making one-sided small talk with the baby while I waited for my drink. There was a woman standing next to me, also waiting for a drink, who reminded me of Ricki, which startled me a bit. She smiled, more in my direction than the baby's. I groaned internally. I cringed at the thought of another night of having a woman persistently hit on me.

"Hi," she said inevitably, still grinning.

Her drink came, and I stood uncomfortably waiting for her to walk away. When she didn't, I politely said, "Hi," and turned to look for my drink.

"What a beautiful baby."

"She sure is, aren't you, honey?"

I was relieved when the bartender appeared with my drink. I smiled at the woman, and walked away.

I traded drinks with Toni.

"Another admirer?" she teased.

"Yes, but of Anabeth, this time," I replied with a smile. Much to my relief, the subject was dropped.

~ ~ ~

Although our town is relatively small, it nevertheless has a healthy and populous gay community. Probably because it is a college town, it is primarily populated by open-minded residents. Along with a handful of gay clubs, we also have a weekly gay newspaper.

It was the most recent issue of that paper that I found open on Toni's kitchen table the following week when I stopped by on my way home from work. The paper was open to the Classified section.

I glanced at Toni, who was across the table, feeding Anabeth. "What's this? Are you looking to buy something?"

"No. I left that there for you. There's something in the Classifieds for you."

My puzzlement was evident, and she grinned as she spooned baby food into Anabeth's mouth. I opened my mouth to ask what she was talking about, but she pre-empted my unvoiced question.

"Look in the 'At A Glance' section under 'Women.'"

Dumbstruck, I scanned the few listings directed at women before seeing the one she was referring to. I glanced through it and saw that the ad was definitely addressed to me. It read:

You: Beautiful blonde at bar at The Gallery AIDS fundraiser. Me: Waiting for a drink at the bar. I commented on the baby you were holding. Yours? Our time together was too fleeting for me to ask, but if there's no other mommy in the picture, I'm interested.

Signed, More Than Curious.

Her contact information was at the bottom of the ad.

I laughed out loud, more out of nervousness than because it was funny.

"I was just flipping through and saw that. I couldn't wait to show you." Toni said. "I saw her talking to you, and I assumed, correctly, that she was interested," she said seriously.

"Yeah, well I thought I'd made it clear to her that I'm not interested." I closed the subject along with the paper.

"Beth, what Bryce said is true, isn't it?" she said hesitantly. "You haven't been with anyone since our break-up."

"Bryce has a well-intentioned, yet nevertheless big mouth," I fired back.

"Uh-huh, he does." She laughed. "But is it true?"

Suddenly unable to find my voice, I nodded. I cleared my throat, lifted my chin, and said defensively, "Yes, it's true."

"Can I ask you why?"

"Why aren't you with someone?" I countered.

She sat back in the chair with a heavy sigh. "I made a conscious decision to direct all of my energy toward Anabeth. I don't want her to have to miss out on anything because she has to share me with someone who might not be here next week. I tried being with Leah, but as soon as I knew I was ready to get pregnant, I ended it with her, because I knew she wasn't someone I wanted to raise a child with, and I knew I didn't love her. For me, having a baby was more important than having a relationship."

She wiped her hands on a towel. "Your turn. It has been almost two years. Why haven't you tried to find someone else?"

I sat silent, not making eye contact.

"It's not worth it. I don't want to hurt anyone else, and I don't want anyone to hurt me. It's not so bad being alone. I have friends who love me."

Toni folded her arms and looked across the table at me, a disapproving frown clear on her face. "I think you need to give it a try, Beth. Why don't you contact this woman?"

I exhaled sharply. "Toni, why are you pushing this? I don't want to contact her. You should know you're the only one I want." The pure truth had come out in a breathless rush. I hadn't intended to say it, and my hand went to my mouth. "I'm sorry. Forget I said that."

"How long have you felt this way?"

I couldn't read her reaction in the least. Flustered and embarrassed, I grabbed my briefcase and then began buttoning my suit jacket.

"Beth, talk to me, please!"

"I have to go, Toni. Maybe we shouldn't see each other for a while so we— so I can sort out my feelings," I sputtered.

"It sounds like you already have yours sorted out. Why won't you talk to me?" she pleaded. I stopped at the door and turned. "Because it seems as though you already have your feelings sorted out too. You've made yourself clear — trying to persuade me to date other people. I don't want to lose the friendship it's taken us so long to build. I have to go."

I drove directly to Laurel's house, which was always the place I ran to when I was upset. I pulled into the driveway and found only Will's car. Sitting silently behind the wheel of my car,

I weighed my options. Either Laurel was inside and Will had used her car, no one was home, or Will was home without his wife. Considering how bad I felt, I opened the car door and went to the front door. Cool air from the open living room window whispered over me as I stepped into the living room, where Will sat in front of the television, beverage in hand. He smiled as I plopped down next to him.

"Where's Laurel?" I asked, praying that he'd say she was upstairs, while knowing that the one car in the driveway probably meant I was out of luck.

"She's at the store. Just left a few minutes ago."

"Damn!"

He looked me over carefully. "Want to tell me what's up?" he asked tentatively.

His dark eyes were boring into me, his look identical to the one Laurel would be wearing had she been there.

"Who said anything's up?"

He set his glass on the coffee table and pointed the remote control at the television, silencing it with the click of a button. "You look frazzled, and you're asking for Laurel. I recognize the signs," he joked, trying to ease my nerves.

I sat quietly, considering whether I should pour out my heart to Will or leave and call Laurel later on. His concern decided me. "I think I've ruined things with Toni. Again." I sighed deeply.

"What happened?"

I recounted the evening's events to him, including the fact that I hadn't wanted to give Toni any indication of how I still felt about her.

He listened intently to the entire tale before he spoke. "What makes you think you've ruined everything?"

"She wants friendship from me, nothing more. She's made that pretty clear. Now that she knows I'm interested in something more, she's going to back off." I shook my head at my stupidity.

"How do you know she doesn't feel the same way?" Will asked.

"Because she's been encouraging me to see other women. That's what she was up to tonight...matchmaking. She's done it before, too."

Will cleared his throat. "Do you want my advice?"

"Maybe you haven't learned everything from Laurel. She doesn't ask, she just gives it," I teased.

He smiled. "Give Toni a break, Beth. This has been a long, crazy road for both of you. Give her a chance to tell you what she's feeling. If her feelings are platonic, then assure her that your emotions won't get in the way of your friendship with her. On the other hand, if you can't set aside your love for her and continuing this relationship is too painful, maybe you should just end it."

He sat back, arms folded, obviously pleased with himself.

I moved closer and rested my head on his shoulder. "You're wonderful. You've managed to make me feel a little better. If Laurel didn't have you, I'd marry you in a second. After the sex change, of course."

He put an arm around my shoulder and turned up the volume on the television, and we sat companionably, watching the rest of the program.

Something in the pit of my stomach was still worrying me, though, and I wasn't sure I would be able to follow through on Will's sage advice.

Chapter Thirty-Three

The following days were excruciating. I had become so accustomed to seeing Toni and Anabeth, that I missed them terribly. I hadn't called Toni as Will had suggested, but what made me feel worse, she hadn't called me.

I was sure that I had scared her off by admitting that she was the only woman I'd ever love. Toni and I had been getting along well over the last few months and, in one short conversation, I had set our relationship back to the point it had been after our relationship dissolved.

I told no one besides Will what had happened, and if my other friends noticed a difference in me, they didn't let on. I immersed myself in my work and tried to forget the pain I had once again caused myself.

A full week passed before I answered my phone and heard Toni's voice on the other end. My heart leapt into my throat, and my palms began to sweat.

"I've left you alone with your thoughts and your feelings and your assumptions for a week. Now will you talk to me?"

"When?"

"Come over for dinner tonight. Anabeth and I miss you, and I have something for you."

My mind raced with the possibilities, both good and bad, and my voice shook a little, but I agreed. "What time do you want me?"

"Come on over right after work, assuming that you are not still working until midnight, of course," she said dryly.

"Ha, ha. I'll be there about six, then."

"Fine. See you then."

The rest of the day dragged and raced at the same time. I was alternately filled with dread and exuberance. Bottom line was, Toni had called, and I was going to see her and Anabeth.

When Toni opened the door, she was holding Anabeth on one hip. Both were smiling, and I took that as an indication that there was a good evening ahead of me.

"Come on out into the kitchen so I can check on dinner.

While Toni occupied herself at the stove, I sat at the table, keeping an eye on Anabeth, who was lurching around the kitchen floor in a walker.

"You know, Beth, you're your own worst enemy when it comes to love," she began, her back toward me as she stirred the contents of a pot on the stove. "You're successful in everything else — your career, your friendships, but when it comes to romantic relationships, you do your best to shoot yourself in the foot."

"What's your point?" I asked, a bit piqued.

Toni put down the spoon and grabbed the latest issue of the gay weekly.

Oh God. Please don't make me read yet another message from More Than Curious, I thought with growing dread.

Toni sat in the chair next to mine and set the paper on the table in front of her.

"What I'm trying to say is..." She took a deep breath and let it out in a rush. "I know I never gave us a chance to talk about...what happened on your birthday. In the first few months, I had so much anger inside that I didn't want to hear anything you had to say, any explanations you might have. And I guess after we patched things up enough to spend time together, I was afraid talking things over would ruin the friendship we had taken so long to rebuild.

"What I didn't realize until last week is that you've been feeling the same way I do." Her face softened, and she appeared relieved.

"I'm sorry, Toni, but I'm not following what you're trying to tell me."

"I can tell. Read this." She flipped through the newspaper, found what she was looking for, and pushed the open paper over to me.

"Toni, this isn't—"

"Please, just read it.

With a sigh of resignation, I scanned the section I knew she wanted me to read, the same personal ads she'd set before me just a week before this whole uncomfortable situation began — *At A Glance.*

My eye was immediately drawn to the ad printed in boldface, but instead of what I had anticipated, I found the following:

Dear More Than Curious: Sorry, but she's taken. Signed, The Other Mommy.

I read the notice twice, and then a third time, before I slowly looked up at Toni.

The confident part of her was smiling, but the unsure part was biting the inside of her lip, afraid of how she hoped I wouldn't react.

"You did this?"

Toni nodded.

"Are you sure?" My voice was a whisper, as if I didn't want to ask the question because I was afraid to hear the answer.

Her eyes bright with tears, she nodded. "I've never stopped loving you, Beth, I just convinced myself that what we had was a one-shot deal. I thought once I lost you, we'd never find our way back to each other. I let my anger and pride keep us apart. I know I was wrong to not try to fix what we had. I've been so unhappy without you, and I want to start over again."

My mouth open and my eyes wide, I stared at Toni. My head swam as I processed her words. *I want to start over again.* Those were the words my damaged heart needed to heal, words I never thought I would hear. Could I be the person I needed to be for Toni? Had all of the time apart taught me what I needed to learn?

"Beth? Did you hear what I said?" Toni frowned, which formed an adorable V between her eyes, something that aging had added to her gorgeous face.

How Still My Love – a contemporary romance

I looked into her eyes, which were questioning. I studied her face, the face I had loved for what seemed like a lifetime — older now, but even more attractive to me than when we had met.

My eyes misted and a slow smile formed on my face. "You're serious? This is what you want? You want to give me another chance?"

My words sounded loud as they left my mouth, and I held my breath, feeling I had stupidly given her a chance to change her mind by putting my doubt into words.

Toni stepped closer and placed her hand on my cheek. "I want to give *us* another chance. Please tell me you want this too, Beth. We've been apart too long."

My emotions whirled and my smile grew. Nothing would keep me from grasping this precious gift. I moved closer to Toni and took her in my arms.

"I never stopped loving you, either. Not for a second. You and Anabeth are everything to me, and I swear I will never, *ever* give you reason to doubt me again."

Toni's sniffles told me she was crying. She tightened her embrace, and whispered, "Thank God."

She leaned away from me and kissed me. It felt new, yet at the same time, as if we hadn't spent a moment apart.

She gazed into my eyes. "I have to get Anabeth fed and bathed before I put her to bed, but will you stay with me tonight?"

She was just inches from my lips, and I whispered, "I'll help. What are mommies for?"

Anabeth cooperated with her mothers' plans for the evening by eating her dinner, and allowing us to bathe her and get her off to bed without a fuss.

We went into the living room and settled together on the sofa. Toni's body pressed against mine, her breath warm on my face. She kissed me softly, starting at my neck and then moving to my mouth. She cupped my face in her hands and looked into my eyes, her desire reflecting my own as she kissed me deeply.

"Anabeth should be asleep by now, so we won't be disturbed," Toni whispered. "Come to bed."

She stood and took my hand, then tugged me with her into the bedroom. She turned on a small lamp near her bed and returned to me with a smile. She lifted my hands to her lips and softly kissed them before removing my clothes, allowing each article to fall to the floor. When I was naked, she undressed and went to the bed, where she turned down the covers and laid down. She beckoned me to her and pulled me down on top of her.

Our kisses began slow and soft and turned deep and desiring. I tasted the inside of her mouth, and she moaned. My mouth moved to her neck, nipping tenderly from her earlobes to her collarbone. Her breathing was ragged as I kissed her breasts, then took each nipple into my mouth. My own breath was coming in short gasps of pent up desire. For nearly two years my body had wanted this woman, and here she was in my arms. The moans coming from her throat were music to my ears.

Toni's hands were in my hair, pulling me closer. Without warning, she turned me onto my back and lay across me. "Let's go slow," she whispered, her breath tickling my ear. "I want this to last all night." She looked into my eyes. "I love you, baby."

I smiled through my tears. "I love you, too."

She kissed me again. She kissed down my entire body and then back up again, until I thought I would lose my mind.

"Please, Toni, I can't wait any longer. Don't make me wait."

She slid down the length of my body, leaving a trail of kisses. A moan escaped my lips as my legs shifted apart. Her tongue felt like silk, pushing me closer to the edge with each stroke. My hands grasped the edge of the bed, tugging with all of my strength, as her fingers slipped into me, one by one.

I tried to hold off, I didn't want the ecstasy to end, but her persistent touch took my breath away. Stars flashed behind my eyes, and I cried out. She slowed but didn't stop, and I stilled her hand with mine. "Toni, Toni, please, that's all I can take for now."

She climbed up to me and met my gaze. "I've missed you."

"Just let me catch my breath. It ain't over yet, honey," I teased.

"Oh, I'm well aware of that." She took my hand and slid it between her legs, smiling at my sharp intake of breath when I felt her wetness.

"Mmm, I've missed you too" I rolled her off of me and onto her stomach, then left a trail of kisses from her neck down to the backs of her knees, before working my way back up her body. Detecting a change in her breathing, I turned her over and moved to her center. It had been two years since I had loved her this way, and yet all the time we'd been apart disintegrated as I touched her.

I moved with Toni, following her rhythm. As she climaxed, she called my name, her body writhing and shuddering before she collapsed beneath me. I moved up to lie beside her and hold her in my arms. I never wanted to leave her side again.

She gazed up into my face. "That was wonderful. I'd almost forgotten how good it is with us."

"Should I be offended?" I asked.

"I said 'almost.'" She laughed and kissed me tenderly.

"We've wasted so much time, Toni. I don't want to be apart from you for a second."

She smiled and cupped my face. "I've come to a conclusion about what happened between us. Tell me what you think." She propped herself up on an elbow and ran her fingers through my hair.

"We met, and almost instantly, we were the typical lesbian couple — living together practically right away. We fell in love before we got to know one another. I think we needed this time apart for each of us to grow and get to the same point in our lives. This time we can make it work, because we've built this on a friendship first. Do you understand what I'm trying to say?"

I thought about it for a few seconds. "I guess I can see what you mean. I just wish we could've gotten to this point without all the pain."

How Still My Love – a contemporary romance

She kissed my fingers and smiled. "It helped me. Pain can be a learning experience too, you know. What matters is that we've found our way back to each other." She took a deep breath and let it out. "You've also resolved things with your parents….well, with your dad. I think that speaks volumes as to how much you've grown."

I squeezed her hand.

"I think your relationship with them…or lack of relationship with them, made you afraid of commitment, and you reacted the only way you knew how. And I made so many mistakes myself."

I opened my mouth to disagree, but Toni placed her hand gently over my lips.

"I did, Beth, I did. I knew you were unhappy, and I just selfishly forged ahead with my plans. I guess I thought you'd adjust to the changes I was making. I promise I will never do that to you again."

I kissed her until our passion flared again. We made love through the night, making plans and promises and more plans. Sleep didn't come until the very early hours, but when it did, it was a sounder sleep than any I'd fallen into in the time we had been apart.

EPILOGUE: THREE YEARS LATER

The entire East Coast was experiencing an unusually mild summer, but none of us minded at all, especially me. The weather was sunny enough for us to have backyard picnics occasionally, and that's what was on the agenda for the day.

I sat at a small table in the backyard of the house Toni and I had bought a year after our reconciliation, not long before we legally married. It wasn't our dream home, as our first home together had been, but we did everything we could to renovate this house to our mutual liking. And, it was perfect for raising kids.

Becca was entertaining Anabeth by pushing her on the backyard swing. Anabeth's screams of delight intermittently pierced the air, while Laurel and I chatted. Will was acting as the man of the house as he grilled our dinner on the other side of the yard. Bryce and Phillip, his partner of two years, stood on one side of a makeshift volleyball net, half-heartedly competing against Kristy and her husband. My dad stood next to Will, overseeing the grilling of the steaks and sipping from a tall glass of iced tea.

Dad loved his iced tea. It was one of the things I had recently learned about him. There were so many things I hadn't had the chance to learn, thanks to my mother and her close-mindedness. I sighed as the realization struck me that I was allowing my mother to ruin the day, and she wasn't even there, except in spirit. My father was a grown man, who was responsible for his own actions. Unlike my mother, he had taken responsibility for having failed me all those years ago, and was doing his best to undo the damage. It took me a long time to accept my father for who he was and forgive him for how he had treated me. Now I was working toward forgetting.

"Momma, look at me! Look how high!" Anabeth squealed, interrupting my musings.

I smiled as I took in her wavy dark hair and the Kool-Aid mustache above her upper lip.

"Yes, honey, I see you. Just be careful!" I fretted aloud.

"I'm watching her, Aunt Beth. Don't worry so much," Becca chided from her place behind the swing.

"I can't believe Anabeth will be going to preschool in the fall." Laurel sighed. "The years are flying by so quickly."

I was sure she was thinking about her own daughters as well as mine. Becca and Kira were speeding toward young adulthood and were at the stage where they were both boy-crazy, something I couldn't relate to in the least.

"I know. I can't believe there's another one on the way." My hand rested on my swollen belly. We were expecting our second child, another girl, in another two months, but Toni teased that I might deliver any day.

I glanced at Toni and saw her watching my hand on my midsection, a beaming smile of pride on her face.

I loved going through everything I had missed during Toni's

pregnancy with Anabeth. The feeling as Toni held me in her arms every night while our baby moved between us was incredible. The hardest part of the pregnancy so far was my hand being so swollen my wedding ring no longer fit. I was temporarily wearing it on a chain around my neck, refusing to relinquish my bond with my wife.

"Is it getting hotter out here, or is it just me?" I asked as Toni moved toward me with a glass of icy lemonade.

"It's just you," Toni and Laurel answered in unison.

"I think this baby has raised my body temperature about twenty degrees," I lamented. "Why was the first one so much easier?"

"Uh, because I had her," Toni teased. "Sit down, and I'll rub your feet."

I sat down in a canvas chair after making Laurel promise she'd help me out of it. Toni handed me the glass of lemonade and parked herself on the lawn, taking my bare feet into her lap.

Shouts of victory came from Kristy's side of the net, and Bryce responded, "That just means that it's time for a cocktail."

Tossing her head back, Laurel laughed out loud as she watched me.

"Do I want to know?" I asked.

"It's just that I never thought the day would come when you'd be barefoot and pregnant."

I didn't find the comment as humorous as she did. "Yeah, well, I'm seeing a lot of things I never thought I'd see. I didn't think Toni and I would find our way back to each other. And I certainly never thought I'd be having a cookout with my dad."

Toni and Laurel both nodded.

"I also never thought I'd have two beautiful women catering to my every need. I could *really* get used to this."

Toni flicked her finger across the bottom of my foot. "Watch it, you can be replaced," she warned.

"Can I?"

Laurel laughed at our banter.

Toni thought for a second, and then said, "Nope. I tried that. It didn't work. No one could replace you."

Across the yard, I could see Will waving smoke from the grill away from his face while he grilled the steaks. Becca was responding to Anabeth's shrieks of "Higher, Becca, higher!" and Toni and Laurel were in a deep discussion about the upcoming semester.

I smiled and sighed deeply, reveling in my happiness and knowing this was how I wanted my life to be, and I would never do anything to risk it again.

Toni lifted my feet and placed them gently on the ground, then rose and walked around behind me. She wrapped her arms around me and nuzzled her face in my hair, tickling my ear with a quick kiss.

"Promise me forever," she whispered, as she had asked me so many years before.

This time, I didn't laugh. I'd never been more serious than when I answered, "Forever, I promise."

Toni walked around to face me and crouched down to my

level. She smiled and kissed me tenderly. "I believe you, my love."

I lifted the wedding ring on the chain around my neck and held it up to her. "All my love, for you and our family, for all of our tomorrows."

Thanks for reading!

Any author will tell you that that greatest honor is to have readers take the time to write a favorable review. If you've enjoyed *How Still My Love*, a brief review on Amazon will help other readers find my work and would be greatly appreciated. Please visit: amazon.com/author/dianemarina.

Also by Diane Marina

- *Landslide*
- *Sisters of the Moon* (When The Clock Strikes Thirteen Anthology)
- *Imperial Hotel*

Follow Diane – Facebook
www.facebook.com/DianeMarinaAuthor

Follow Diane – Twitter
@diane_marina

Contact Diane
diane.marina@ymail.com

Printed in Great Britain
by Amazon